"Tell n
"I know
"That's
behind her shoulders and foot again. "Why don't you tell me something I don't know?"

Nick clenched his hands into fists and crossed his arms. Shaking his head, he said, "You have no idea what this man is capable of."

"If you tell me, then I'd know wouldn't I?"

He ground his teeth and sighed as his irritation grew. "It's getting late. I'll walk you back to your room." He turned on his heel and picked up the water bottles, napkin and the sandwich wrapper, dumping them into the poolside trash can before facing her again.

"So that's it? You won't tell me anything?"

"No. I *can't* tell you anything. Not yet."

Cali looked away, took in a deep breath and walked past him out of the pool gate. He let her lead the way back to her rented room. Stopping in front of the door, she wrapped her arms around herself and studied her toes.

Nick slipped the key into the slot and turned it, opening the door an inch. When she moved to step inside, he caught her slender arm in his grasp. "Stop snooping, Cali. Don't put yourself at risk."

Her full lips tightened. "I can take care of myself."

"Yeah? That's probably what Serena thought, too."

A brief flash of pain crossed her eyes before they became guarded.

"Listen, Cali, I'm only trying to keep you safe. It's my duty to protect you."

Renewed determination swirled in her eyes along with a spark of anger. "Yeah? Well, don't do me any favors. It was your duty to protect Serena, too. And look what happened to her."

Night Waves

by

Wendy Davy

This is a work of fiction. Names, characters, places, and incidents either are the product of the author's imagination or are used fictitiously, and any resemblance to actual persons living or dead, business establishments, events, or locales, is entirely coincidental.

Night Waves

COPYRIGHT © 2009 by Wendy Davy

All rights reserved. No part of this book may be used or reproduced in any manner whatsoever without written permission of the author or The Wild Rose Press except in the case of brief quotations embodied in critical articles or reviews.
Contact Information: info@thewildrosepress.com

Cover Art by *Nicola Martinez*

White Rose Publishing
A division of The Wild Rose Press
PO Box 708
Adams Basin, NY 14410-0706
Visit us at www.whiterosepublishing.com

Publishing History
First White Rose Edition, 2009
Print ISBN 1-60154-645-9

Published in the United States of America

Dedication

For the victims of violent crime, and their families.

In Loving Memory of:
Mattie and Odeon Bloodgood

Praise for Wendy Davy

On Drake's Retreat:

"The story flowed so well I couldn't believe when it ended...It is a great read, fun and well worth your time."

~ Brenda, The Romance Studio

"*Drake's Retreat* is a well-written look at the opportunity one has to overcome their circumstances when they are willing to step outside their comfort zone...Read this inspirational romance for a warm-hearted look at the transformation that takes place when someone places God at the center of his or her life."

~ Night Owl Romance

On A Matter of Trust:

"This is the first book I have read by Wendy Davy and I have to say that I would look for more of her books as she writes very well and her plot line keeps the reader hooked...It is worth treating yourself to this one..."

~Mary, A Romance Review

Remember the Lord, who is great and awesome, and fight for your brothers, your sons and your daughters, your wives and your homes.
~ *Nehemiah 4:14 (NIV)*

Chapter One

"Go home Ms. Stevens." Sheriff Nick Justice let out a long, exaggerated breath. "If you want to help your friend, trust me to handle the investigation." His resolute gaze held hers without the slightest hint of contempt, but she detected a flicker of impatience run across the dark-blue depths.

Cali Stevens tightened her grip on the hard, wooden armrests of the hard, wooden chair she sat in. She had no doubt the Sheriff of Coral Isle intended the visitors in his office to keep their conversations, or as in her case, their pleas, short and to the point. She glanced around the office. Her gaze touched the bare walls, the spotless tiled floor, and his sparsely occupied desk. Only the barest of essentials earned a place there—a computer, telephone, several neatly stacked file folders, and a half-empty coffee cup. She assumed Sheriff Justice's personality reflected the office in which they both sat. Hard, well-organized, and no-nonsense.

When she remained seated, he sat forward in

his swivel chair and pinched the bridge of his nose with his thumb and forefinger. "Listen, Ms. Stevens..." Weariness seeped through his voice.

"Cali." She hoped he might see her as more than an outsider if he called her by her first name.

"Cali." He lifted his head and braced his hands on the edge of the desk. "I assure you, we're doing everything possible to find Ms. Taylor. Now if you'll excuse me." He stood, keeping his tight gaze directed at her.

She shook her head, causing it to ache with growing intensity. "No. I won't. I came here for answers, and I'm not leaving without them."

He placed his hands on his hips. One rested directly on a set of handcuffs that he looked more than willing and able to use. A muscle in his jaw twitched, the only outward indication of his failing patience. "I understand your concern."

"My concern? Serena Taylor is my roommate, and my best friend. I've known her for over ten years. She's like a sister to me. Concern doesn't begin to describe how I feel." Her fingers started going numb from her grip on the chair, so she lessened the pressure and took a deep breath, trying to calm her nerves. "I just want to know where she is. I need to know she's OK."

"Regardless of what you may think, Ms. Stevens, I do understand what you want and I understand why. But, I cannot give you details of an ongoing investigation."

"I answered your questions. Now it's your turn to answer mine." She fought to keep her voice from cracking and to keep from showing any signs of weakness. "I want, no, I *need* to know what you know about her disappearance."

He hesitated before crossing the office to ease the door shut, blocking out any potential eavesdroppers. A hint of concern crossed his angled features as he turned and ran a hand over his dark, close-cropped hair. His eyes softened as he admitted, "We believe she's been abducted." His low voice made its way across the now quiet room, filling her with terror like she had never known.

"No." She stood on shaky legs and rubbed her damp palms together as tears threatened to emerge. "Why would someone..." She let her words falter as she imagined many horrible reasons for a young, beautiful woman to be abducted. She hugged her arms around her middle. "What makes you think she's been abducted? Do you have evidence? Witnesses?" She tilted her head to the side, biting her lower lip to keep it from trembling.

Sheriff Justice remained motionless. "I can't reveal any details of an open investigation. But as I said, we are doing everything possible to find her."

Cali ignored his attempt at reassurance. "I knew something was terribly wrong when she didn't come home from her vacation. I knew she wouldn't stay on Coral Isle longer than she'd planned without calling and letting me know."

He placed his hands on his hips again, looked to the floor and slowly shook his head. After a few moments, he lifted his eyes. "I'm sorry."

His softly offered words drew her out of her panic, out of her paralyzing fear. She straightened her spine. "You sound like you've already given up on her." Lifting her chin, she filled her lungs with fresh oxygen and strengthened her voice along with her resolve. "Let me tell you something. I will not leave this island until she's found. So, if you want me to go home you'd better get busy."

He broadened his stance and dropped his hands. "Let me tell *you* something." His voice took on a tone of authority, all traces of softness instantly gone. "I don't give up. Ever. I have this investigation under control. You," he pointed a steady finger at her, "need to go home and leave the investigation to the professionals."

She lifted her chin. "I am a professional."

He scoffed as the corner of his lips turned up into a slight, mockery of a smile, "I'd hardly call an amateur reporter from Brookstone, North Carolina—grand total population of five hundred thirty-two—a professional."

Cali heard her own intake of breath as heat bruised her cheeks. She should not be surprised about his opinion; she had received the same skeptical reaction many times before, mostly from overbearing, egotistical men. She lifted her chin higher, refusing to let him intimidate her. "I'm good at what I do."

"Yes, well, *Ms. Stevens*," he pronounced her last name clearly, as if they had taken a step back into formalities, "so am I." He started to open the door but the phone interrupted him. He walked to his desk and picked it up. After answering, he placed a hand over the receiver. "Excuse me. This is important."

"Remember, Serena's important, too." Cali forced her unwilling legs to move, one step in front of the other. She opened the door and walked out without looking back. The once-clear voices of the officers and visitors in the waiting area now sounded like distant mumbles, undecipherable through the blood rushing through her ears.

She spotted the restroom across the busy office and headed directly for it. She shoved open the door and stepped inside, thanking God no one occupied the small room with the single toilet. She flipped the lock, and then willingly gave up what was left of her meager breakfast.

Several minutes passed as she ran cold water over her hands, and splashed her face and neck. Somewhat refreshed, she turned off the water and looked into the mirror. She found a distant relation to her normal appearance. Her faintly tanned skin had taken on a pallor with a sickly green tint, and it wasn't only from the fluorescent lighting that flickered overhead. Her long blonde hair hung in tangled waves down her shoulders, looking as twisted and mangled as she felt inside.

On an impulse, she fished her cell phone out of her purse and tried calling Serena's number as she had numerous times in the past few hours. She listened to the voicemail pick up immediately, indicating the phone was still turned off. Serena never turned off her cell phone. Cold chills ran up Cali's arms at the disturbing thought.

She snapped the phone closed as the feeling of complete and utter helplessness churned her already rolling stomach. She searched through her purse for breath mints, but dropped the package three times before she managed to release two of the small pieces. She tried to calm her shaking hands, but feared the quivering was nowhere near an end.

"This cannot be happening," her voice sounded weak, echoing across the small, tiled room. Sudden anger brushed past her fears. If there was one thing she had no tolerance for, it was weakness. A new determination surged forth, along with a shot of adrenaline into her veins. She came to Coral Isle looking for answers, and she refused to leave without them, regardless of what Sheriff Justice demanded.

She swung the bathroom door open with so much force that she nearly knocked down an older woman trying to gain entrance. After giving a brief apology and holding the door open for the slight woman, Cali headed straight for the row of chairs lining the front wall. She would give the sheriff one more chance to answer her questions, and if he didn't satisfy her need to know what was going on, she would dig in her heels and do some investigating of her own. She sat in one of the gray, plastic molded chairs prepared to wait as long as necessary to speak with him again.

****

Sheriff Nick Justice drank the last of his cold, stale coffee, hoping the small burst of caffeine would help fight the tension headache he'd had brewing since Cali Stevens walked into his office. He already felt responsible for the missing woman, but after hearing the desperation in Ms. Stevens's voice, his sense of responsibility multiplied.

After she had left his office, his conversation on the phone had been brief, and he had spent half an hour with his door closed and head bowed in prayer. He needed guidance big time on this one. He prayed this last disappearance would not confirm his worst fears, but in his heart, he already knew the answer. A serial rapist had decided to use his small, tourist-based island as a hunting ground.

His phone buzzed, indicating Helen, the dispatch officer, wanted to speak with him. Jerked out of his thoughts, he pressed the button. "Yes?" he asked, but he had already guessed what the motherly woman intended to say.

"You need to get some lunch in you, Nick. You can't take care of others if you…"

"Don't take care of yourself," he finished. Despite his stress-induced headache, he smiled into the speaker. Helen always kept him on track. "I'm heading out now."

"One more thing…" The hesitation in her voice, an unnatural and rare occurrence coming from Helen, made Nick's heart lurch. Whatever she had to say, it could not be good. She continued in her sweet southern drawl, "Ms. Stevens hasn't left yet. She's waiting to speak with you again."

Nick didn't respond. He sat back in his chair, groaned, and ran a hand over his face. Although he could not blame the woman for wanting answers, he had a job to do, and it didn't involve letting an innocent woman put herself in danger. The sooner he convinced her to leave, the better off she would be.

Nick stood, grabbing his pair of sunglasses from inside the desk drawer. He double-checked the pistol holstered at his hip and headed for the door. His intentions to placate Ms. Stevens in order to convince her to leave flew right out of his mind when he opened the door and locked eyes with her. A new determination glittered in the clear-blue depths, and her rigid posture spoke volumes. There would be no placating this woman.

He slipped on his sunglasses and headed out of the front door. Knowing she would follow, he held the door open so it wouldn't slam into her. As he stepped outside, the scent of the salty sea air surrounded him. It normally comforted him, but today, the heavy humidity accompanying it took away its soothing effects. The onslaught of stifling August heat made Nick's headache escalate from mildly annoying to downright nauseating. He walked to his white truck with the words "Sheriff, Coral Isle" printed in bold lettering on the side and leaned against the driver's side door, crossing his arms over his chest.

"I seem to recall asking you to leave," his abrupt words reflected his down-spiraling mood.

Cali dug in her purse and pulled out a pair of sunglasses. Perching them on the bridge of her nose, she peeked over the rims. "I seem to recall asking you for information regarding Serena's disappearance." She lifted the designer glasses higher, effectively shielding her eyes from the sun—and him.

Nick looked at her petite figure, and resisted his natural protective instinct that urged him to take it easy on her. "You're a reporter. You should know I can't give you information about an ongoing investigation." He used his gruff "cop" voice hoping to dissuade her.

"You don't intimidate me." She raised her chin

high.

Cali put on a brave show, but he caught sight of her pulse pounding at the base of her slender throat. Despite her brave appearance, she was scared, if not of him then of the circumstances she found herself in, and to be honest, she had every right to be.

"How long did it take you to drive here?"

"Three hours. Why?"

He looked to the bright, mid-day sun then back at her. "Good. That will give you plenty of daylight hours to drive back home. If you get started now, you'll be back in time for dinner." Nick watched a sigh heave her chest, and then directed his gaze back to a more respectable position.

"Will you at least tell me why you think she's been abducted? Do you have evidence to support it? Was she seen with someone before she disappeared? A man?" She fired the questions in quick succession.

He shook his head. "I can't tell you. Not yet."

"Then what can you tell me?"

He raised his voice a notch, trying to drive home his point. "I can tell you to go home. It would be best for all of us."

"Best for all of us? You mean easiest don't you? Easiest for you."

Even standing with her hands balled into fists and irritation showing through her tense facial expression, she looked as dangerous as a kitten. It was impossible to protect every single woman on the island, but he felt the overwhelming need to protect this one. This one would be a prime target for his suspect. A woman. Alone. Virtually defenseless.

He gritted his teeth and swore under his breath. "There's nothing easy about this whole situation. And yes, you are making things more difficult. Right now, I'm hungry, hot, and have a killer headache. I suggest you get on your way before I decide to arrest you for something."

She must have believed his threat, because she

backed away a step. "I should tell you. I never give up either. Ever." She spun on her heel and marched to her silver-blue economy car. She jerked the door open, climbed in and drove away without looking back.

Deputy Owen stepped outside and sauntered over to stand beside Nick. "She's cute." His long, narrow face held a hint of a smile.

Beautiful, Nick corrected the observation in silence as the car disappeared, heading in the opposite direction from the only bridge leading off the island.

"I had a feeling she'd show up here. When she called yesterday to report that Ms. Taylor hadn't returned home, she knew the answers to every question I asked about her friend. They must be close."

"Apparently they are. She's not leaving." His gaze sought Owen. "Find out where she's staying. I'm going to keep a close eye on her."

Another brief smile flitted across Deputy Owen's lips. "Yes sir."

Owen left Nick standing in the sweltering heat, wondering how to manage locating Ms. Taylor while keeping Ms. Stevens and the rest of the single women on his island safe.

Chapter Two

Cali blamed the blast of cold air-conditioning coming from the dashboard vents for the tears in her eyes. Admitting they came from frustration or fear, would be another sign of weakness. She swiped at the wet spots on her cheeks and focused on the road.

She drove aimlessly for several minutes, but her stomach rumbled and fatigue pulled at her, reminding her she couldn't roam around all day without a destination. She needed a place to rest, a place to settle in and devise a plan. She remembered, from glancing briefly at the map of Coral Isle, the main beach road circled the island, and various other roads created a maze of back streets through the interior.

Assuming she would find the majority of the hotels on the main beach road, which someone had unimaginatively named, *The Beach Road*, Cali fought the heavy traffic and found her way to it.

She caught glimpses of the sparkling ocean and tourist-lined beaches as she drove. Cottages, hotels and an occasional public-beach-access parking lot dotted the shoreline. Families carrying toys, towels and chairs darted across the road at various places on their way to the beach. She came to a complete stop to let one family pass. A mother carrying a squiggly child on her hip and holding an older child's hand smiled in Cali's direction, while the father brought up the rear as he lugged a large red and white cooler across the road behind him.

Their lives appeared so normal that it seemed surreal to think of someone disappearing, someone being abducted in such a family-oriented environment. But Serena had been abducted. Cali's smile vanished, and she refocused on the purpose for her visit to the island.

She continued to search for a place with an available room. So far, she had only seen "No Vacancy" signs on each of the hotels. She passed by various shops and restaurants, and a small library that sat nestled off to the right side of the road. Numerous souvenir stores displayed brightly colored T-shirts and skimpy bathing suits, and a wide variety of floats decorated the windows.

Cali searched for miles before spotting a motel across the road from the beach claiming a vacancy. The condition of the old motel turned her initial relief into apprehension as she turned from the main road and drove slowly onto the graveled drive. She shielded her eyes from the glare of the afternoon sun and parked in front of the motel's office, which provided enough shade to see clearly through the windshield. She let the engine idle as she looked over the aging dwelling.

A bright orange neon sign stood posted in the filmy window warning guests no pets were allowed. The door to the office stood propped open by an aluminum beach chair, and a large fan blocked more than half of the entryway. Her eyes automatically darted to the long row of rooms lined to the right, searching for window air-conditioner units. Each room had one. She let out a breath in relief. With the temperatures soaring close to one-hundred degrees, combined with the humidity, she could not imagine staying in a room without bottled air.

She scanned the motel's exterior. Dingy brown

strips of paint peeled from the doors, and the faded accent color of pea-green along the windowsills and doorframes looked to be in no better shape. She wondered if the owners of the establishment had repainted it since it was built, obviously some time in the nineteen-seventies.

As an avid fan of brand name, interior corridor hotels with room service, Cali found this place as appealing as an old cardboard box. But, considering that the Sea Urchin appeared to be the only motel left on the island with a vacancy, she was afraid to pass it up.

Cali reluctantly stepped out into the stifling heat and walked into the office. She held back a few negative comments when the aging owner, who appeared to be in no better shape than the motel, told her she would have to pay for a three-night minimum stay.

After checking in, she parked her car directly in front of her assigned room and unloaded her duffle bag, suitcase, laptop and pillow. When she slipped the key into the door, tagged clearly with the room number twenty-one, she thought wistfully of the key cards most hotels now used. Somehow, those plastic cards with no identifying room number seemed more secure than an old-fashioned cut key.

Ignoring her sudden unease, she stepped into the dim, musty room, lugging her property with her. When she flipped on the lights, her gaze landed on the two beds, and she immediately wondered if anyone had bothered to wash the quilts within the last year.

With an uncontrolled shiver, she closed the door and ripped the covers from the beds, stuffing them into a corner. Glancing under the top sheet of the bed nearest the door, Cali discovered two small gnat-type creatures lying dead on the bottom sheet. She turned and peeled the top sheet off the other bed. This time, she only found one dead bug in between the sheets. With a heavy sigh, she flicked the bug's miniature carcass off the linens and tossed her belongings on the double-bug bed.

"No wonder this place had a vacancy." She circled her temples with her fingertips, trying to ease the ache pulsing through her head. She looked toward the bathroom and groaned, deciding to avoid that room until it was necessary to venture in there.

An overwhelming feeling of isolation blanketed her as she sat in silence for the first time since waking this morning and making the hasty decision to come to Coral Isle, North Carolina. She grabbed her cell phone and flipped it open. Thankful to see a full set of bars across the top, she punched in the numbers she knew by heart and settled back against the set of pillows lining the thin, ailing headboard.

"Shoot." A gravelly male voice came across the line.

Cali almost wept in relief when hearing the familiar word come from the familiar voice. "You never have liked saying 'hello' have you, Dad?"

Donald Stevens's voice softened. "With every hello there has to be a goodbye. And you know how I hate goodbyes."

She smiled, closed her eyes and replied, "I'll never figure you out."

"Neither will your mother, and she's been trying for years."

Laughter trickled from her lips. "I know. Speaking of Mom, have you told her yet?"

"Told her you up and left town this morning without a word to her? You're kidding, right? I figured I'd let you tell her. My old bones don't handle sleeping on the couch the way they used to."

"Fair enough." She shifted lower on the bed, leaned back, and bumped her head against the thin headboard, causing a deeper throb to settle into her skull. She lifted her hand to rub the sore spot. "Just have Mom call me when she gets a chance."

"I will." His voice turned serious, "Have you found out anything about Serena yet?"

She took in a deep breath and let it out slowly. "A little. I stopped by the sheriff's station as soon as I arrived. Sheriff Justice thinks she's been abducted."

"Abducted?"

Cali pictured her father in his cluttered office at the Brookstone Herald with his gray-streaked eyebrows drawn together, and his hand rubbing his jaw as he often did when receiving worrisome news. "I practically begged him to tell me why he thinks it, but he won't. He says he can't reveal details of an ongoing investigation. He has also made it clear he doesn't want me getting involved."

"If someone has kidnapped Serena, you could be putting yourself in danger if you go looking for her. I agree with the sheriff, you should stay out of it. But that's not going to stop you is it?"

"You know it won't. I have to be here for Serena, but I'll be careful."

"Wait a sec." Muffled words came over the line as if he'd put his hand over the receiver. A moment later he said, "I've got to go. Mrs. Welsby is stirring up trouble again."

"I thought you had her banned from the building?"

"I did. She's trying to beat down the front door with her cane. Seems she's disagreeing with the words of wisdom your mother's given in the advice column again."

"Don't be too hard on Mrs. Welsby. She must be in her mid-eighties by now, and who can blame her for being upset? Mom's not always tactful in the way she gives advice."

A chuckle escaped before he said, "You're telling me, kid."

"Dad?"

"Yes, hon'?"

"Will you pray for Serena?"

"I have been. For both of you."

"Thanks." Cali disconnected the call and took a moment to say a few prayers, too.

Refusing to succumb to the pain throbbing in her head, she ignored the temptation to close her eyes and rest. Instead, she pulled a map of Coral Isle out of her suitcase along with a notepad, pencil and a stick of gum. Popping the gum into her mouth, hoping to ease her aching stomach, she began to scribble ideas of where to start searching first.

As possibilities reeled through her mind, she kept coming back to thoughts of the sheriff and his insistence that she return home. Although Sheriff Justice had more resources and more manpower, Cali had an edge he didn't have. She knew Serena personally. Sheriff Justice had the answers to the questions the deputy had asked her. *Does Serena have a boyfriend? Tell me about her past relationships? Has she ever been known to take off for a few days? Does she frequent bars?* The list of questions seemed endless at the time, but now, thinking back on her answers, there was much more she could tell him about Serena's quirks and habits.

Cali picked up her cell phone and placed a call to the sheriff's office. It couldn't hurt to let Sheriff Justice know a few more things about Serena.

A woman with a deep country accent answered the phone, "Sheriff's office."

"This is Cali Stevens. I was in the office earlier today..."

"I remember you. I'm so sorry about your friend, dear," the woman's voice held genuine concern in it.

"Thank you. I'd like to speak with the sheriff, please."

"He's out to lunch. May I take a message?"

Out to lunch? A sudden, unexpected tide of anger swept over Cali. She wanted to ask why he was not out looking for Serena, and why he was not scouring the streets searching for clues. Who did he think he was taking a lunch break?

"No message." Deciding to save her comments for the man himself, she gritted her teeth and closed the phone before she said any of her thoughts aloud. The rational side of her understood the sheriff needed to eat, but the emotional side wanted to tear into him for not spending every waking moment searching for Serena.

Anger combined with rising anxiety and gave her the momentum she needed to ignore her rumbling stomach, achy head, and issues with Coral Isle's sheriff. Deciding not to waste any more time or energy worrying about what the law was doing to find Serena, Cali grabbed her purse and keys and headed for the door, determined to find her best friend on her own.

She found the oceanfront cottage Serena had rented using directions printed from the Internet. Located four miles south of the motel, it took less than ten minutes to get there. A silver SUV sat parked in the carport under the two-story home, indicating another family had already rented it for the week. Saying a quick prayer for courage, Cali parked behind the vehicle, took a deep breath, and climbed from her car with her pulse racing.

The blast of late-afternoon heat hit her first, and the aroma of steaks sizzling on the grill hit her next. Children laughed nearby, and the cheerful noises mixed with the sounds of the waves crashing into the surf. She walked under the stilted home, rounded the side of the cottage and nearly ran into a man grilling the steaks she'd caught the scent of a moment ago.

Pasting a smile on her face, she ignored the heat and her jangled nerves and said, "Hello. I'm Cali Stevens." She held her hand out in greeting.

The middle-aged man shot her an irritated look before poking the steaks with a pair of tongs. "What is it now?"

"Pardon me?"

Cali let her hand drop to her side.

"If you're with the law, I've already told you I don't know anything about what happened to that lady."

Cali swallowed, and tried to keep her breathing even and controlled. "How about we go over it one more time?" She wondered if she could get into trouble by letting the man think she was an officer, but she took the chance anyway. After all, she hadn't identified herself as one.

He let out a heavy sigh and pierced her with his deep-set eyes. His bushy eyebrows drew together as he said, "When me and my family checked in a few hours ago, the tow truck was hauling the lady's car away. You guys had already taken all of her stuff and dusted for prints. Which, may I point out, left a mess all over the place. The cleaning people are on their way, and I ain't paying them to clean up."

"Besides the fingerprint dust, were there any signs of a struggle? Did anything else look out of place?"

"Not unless you count the sink full of dirty dishes and leftover food in the refrigerator. Look, I don't know what you people want from me." He let out a loud sigh.

Cali held her ground, despite the man's growing irritation. "Have you seen anyone suspicious in the neighborhood?"

"I wouldn't know. It took me an hour to unload my stuff, and another hour to arrange for someone to agree to come and clean up the mess left behind. Meanwhile, two sets of officers have stopped by to ask me questions. All I know is, I paid a bundle for this place and so far, I haven't been able to enjoy it yet with all of you parading through." He waved his hands around. "Looking for what, I don't know."

Cali took a step back as the man's rounded face

turned varying shades of red.

"Harold!" A woman's voice came from the deck above their heads.

"I'm coming." The man plopped the sizzling steaks on a plate and turned off the grill. He looked at Cali and wiped beads of sweat from his brow. "I don't have any information about the lady who's gone missing. You'd better get on your way." He turned and stomped up the steps, the boards creaking and groaning under his hefty weight.

The sliding glass door opened and shut before Cali dared let out the breath she had been holding. "That went well." She placed the palm of her hand on her forehead, praying she would still find some tidbit of information that would help lead her to Serena.

When she opened her eyes, she looked around the shaded carport. Numerous stilts held the home far above the ground, designed to preserve the cottage in case of a high water storm surge. An outdoor shower claimed the corner near the downstairs entrance, and a water hose sat coiled up attached to a spigot. A few plastic buckets, shovels and other toys lay in a heap beside the cottage. A layer of sand covered the cement driveway, thicker in some areas where the wind had driven the dunes inland. Several sets of footprints led from the SUV to the cottage stairs, but the possibility of gaining evidence from the shoe imprints would have been destroyed with the new renter's arrival. She only hoped the sheriff had found some sort of useful evidence in time.

Cali turned to head back to her car and spotted something lying partially submerged in the sand at the end of the driveway. She walked over to it and discovered the tip of a piece of paper. She carefully pinched the edge and lifted it. A picture of a black and white lighthouse appeared on the side of the rectangular paper. Cali read the lettering on the front, "Coral Isle Lighthouse admission. Wednesday, August 14th." Her heart leapt. Serena had been here that day last week. She scanned the rest of the ticket, and her breath caught as she whispered, "Admission for two." Serena had gone to the lighthouse, and she had not been alone.

With a pounding heart, Cali climbed into her car intending to head straight for the lighthouse, but soon realized she had no idea where to find it. At the corner of the beach road, she stopped and let the engine idle. She could tell Sheriff Justice about the ticket stub, but she was afraid he would try to keep her from going there and asking the staff questions. Deciding she would like to have a chance to check into the lighthouse personally, Cali made a right turn, heading back to the motel to check the phone book for the Coral Isle Lighthouse's location.

Driving back, Cali's thoughts ran through a maze of possibilities. Who could Serena have gone to the lighthouse with? As far as Cali knew, Serena didn't have any friends coming to visit during her vacation. Had she met someone? Had that someone kidnapped her?

A horn blew, jerking Cali out of her thoughts. She looked up, barely in time to stop at a red light. Her hands shook, and she gripped the steering wheel tighter. "Stay focused, Cali, or you won't be able to find Serena." The rest of the drive back she stayed alert and forced herself to pay attention to the road.

When she arrived at her motel, she rushed in and found the phone book. Flipping through the pages with shaky hands, she found and circled the number to the lighthouse. She dialed and waited for someone to pick up, but a message came over the line. *"We're sorry; the Coral Isle Lighthouse is closed on Mondays. Please call back."* Cali hung up. Her heart sank at the unexpected delay. She flopped onto the bed as the initial rush of adrenaline from finding the ticket dissipated, leaving her completely drained.

She closed her eyes and took deep, calming breaths, promising herself she would check into it first thing in the morning. She explored the options of what she could do with the remainder of the day, but came up blank as exhaustion claimed her. She hadn't eaten and her stomach rumbled in protest, but too tired to do anything about it, she curled on her side and drifted to sleep.

By the time Cali woke, the sun had set and faint moonlight seeped into the motel's small window. She groped through the darkness and flipped on the bedside lamp. As her eyes adjusted, her mind kicked into high gear again, and thoughts of Serena's whereabouts caused the tension in her muscles to come back in force.

Yawning and stretching, Cali climbed from the bed, stepped to the window, and spotted the calm water in the illuminated pool. It looked refreshing, and it only took a moment for her to decide a swim was what she needed.

Chapter Three

Cali stepped out of the air-conditioned room and the thick humidity slammed into her. The salty air clung to her skin and sand rubbed between her toes as she walked across the parking lot to the small, deserted pool. Dropping her towel on a white, plastic lounger, she tucked the room key safely inside the folds.

Sliding into the pool, she noticed the nightlights illuminating her form under the clear water, making her self-conscious, and glad she was the only one in the pool. Cali ducked her head under the refreshing water and swam as far as she dared without taking a breath. Popping out of the water and catching a fresh lungful of air, she continued swimming across the length of the bean-shaped pool. She let the movements calm her and stretch out her tension-filled muscles.

As her energy depleted, she slowed and looked into the star speckled sky. Floating on her back, she let the familiarity of the rising moon comfort her.

"You called?" a deep voice sounded above her head.

Cali nearly swallowed a mouthful of water. She jerked upright and twisted around. Sheriff Justice stood at the edge of the pool, peering down with a white bag stuffed under the crook of his arm. She lifted her eyebrows, trying to make sense of what he said.

"You called asking for me at the station earlier."

Cali remembered placing the call to the sheriff, and she remembered the kind woman answering the call, but could not remember why she had called.

The pool lights reflected off his face, flickering on the wide jaw-line and angled features. A mirthful smile replaced the grim line she had seen on his lips earlier, and the furrow in his brow had disappeared, creating a magnificent view. Completely at a loss for words, Cali simply stared at his handsome face.

"Remember me?"

"Uh...O-of course I do," she sputtered.

His smile broadened. "Sorry I couldn't call you back earlier. We had a beach rescue that took several hours to resolve. I'm on my way home now, and I thought I'd stop by and see what you called about."

"OK," she answered, but she still couldn't remember specifically why she called. Feeling like a bumbling idiot, she closed her mouth and ducked under the water. She wracked her brain as she sprang from the side of the pool and swam underwater, trying to come up with the answer. Lifting her head, she blamed exhaustion for not remembering.

Sheriff Justice followed and met her at the shallow end of the pool. After wiping the dripping water from her eyes, she grasped the edge and waylaid his question with one of her own. "How did you know where to find me?"

"It's a small island. It wasn't hard." He shrugged as if the answer didn't matter. "I brought drinks and a sub-sandwich. You can have half of the sub."

Cali started to shake her head, but when he sat on one of the lounge chairs and pulled out the sandwich, the smell of hot pepperoni, salami and melted cheeses made her mouth water.

"You need to eat." Sheriff Justice leaned forward and handed half of the sandwich and a napkin to her. He settled into the lounger and took a big bite of the other half.

She didn't argue. "Thanks." She leaned forward to keep any crumbs from landing in the water and sunk her teeth into it, savoring the strong, salty taste. After a few bites, guilt swarmed through her. Serena was probably hungry and scared, while she swam in a pool and ate dinner next to a handsome sheriff. She set down the sandwich on the napkin and dusted the crumbs from her hands.

"Not eating won't help you find her."

Cali's gaze automatically shot to his. He had read her mind perfectly.

"You have to take care of yourself. Or, you can't take care of anyone else." He said the words smoothly, as if he spoke or heard them often.

"I understand the concept. But, it's hard when I feel like I should be out there searching for her."

"I have people out there searching. Trust me to do my job, Cali."

She didn't want to start an argument now that he appeared to be in a more relaxed state than he was in at the office, so she kept her tone neutral. "It's not about trusting you or anyone else. It's about me doing what I can do to find her. I can't sit back idly wondering what's happening to her."

"You've already helped by answering Deputy Owen's questions, and mine."

Her eyes widened. "That's why I called you. I wanted to give you more information about Serena."

"What kind of information?" He took another large bite of his sandwich.

She lifted one shoulder. "I know her. I could help you in deciding where to look."

"Where we look is determined by the evidence we find."

"So, where has the evidence led you so far?" She

asked as she began eating again.

A slow smile spread across his lips, but his features became guarded. "Nice try. Do I need to keep reminding you I can't tell you the details?"

"Can't or won't?" She shoved away from the edge of the pool to tread water. When his eyes roamed over the length of her, she remembered the pool lights acted like spotlights on her body. Embarrassed, she swam back to the edge.

Sheriff Justice looked away as if caught doing something he shouldn't, finished the last bite of his dinner, crumpled the paper wrapper into a ball and set it aside. "If I think you might have information about her that would help in a specific circumstance, I'll call you."

"Did you know Serena's a vegetarian?"

He didn't answer.

"Did you know she likes to go horseback riding?"

He still didn't answer.

"Did you know she enjoys sitting on the beach at night and watching the stars come out?"

"Cali." He leaned forward, laced his fingers together and lowered his voice, "I understand what you're trying to do, and I appreciate it. But, we have information you don't have."

"And I have information you don't have. Why won't you let me help?"

A jaw muscle twitched. "Tell you what. Write down everything you know about her. Things you think will help us find her. Drop it by the station tomorrow, and I'll take a look at it."

"I can do that. But it's still not the same. If you take me with you—"

"You don't give up do you?" He unlaced his fingers and leaned back, crossing his arms. "Taking you with me is not an option."

Convinced she had reached an impasse with him, she redirected the conversation. "I went to the cottage today."

"The cottage?" He took a swig from a bottle of water while passing an unopened one to her.

Cali took the offered drink, and then drank half of it when she discovered how thirsty she had become. "The cottage Serena rented."

Sheriff Justice's brow furrowed as he bolted from his seat, took a step toward her, and held his hand out. A grim line of determination slid across his lips. "You need to get out of the pool. It's time we had a serious discussion."

"Fine by me." Cali lifted her hand.

Nick secured her by the wrist. He lifted her out easily with one arm, and set her directly in front of him. The pool water ran in rivulets down her skin, tempting his eyes to follow their descent. He already had a good idea of how well she filled out the swimsuit she wore from seeing her in the water. But now, with mere inches separating them, there was no room for doubt. She looked amazing.

"Sheriff?" she asked as she crossed her arms.

Broken out of his trance, he turned and grabbed her beach towel from the chair. Her room key dropped out and clattered to the concrete. Nick tossed the towel to her and turned to pick up the key, giving himself a moment for a mental shake.

Coral Isle's recent abductions gave him enough to worry about without adding any complications to the mix, and his attraction to Cali Stevens was definitely a complication. Clenching his jaw, he tucked the key into his pocket and turned back to face her. He crossed his arms and set his feet wide apart, trying to look more intimidating than he felt.

"You went snooping around Serena's rental cottage?"

"Not snooping. Investigating." She tucked the towel around her, tilted her chin higher and tapped her right foot.

Nick took a step forward. She retreated. One more inch, and she would be in the pool. "You put up a brave front Cali. But, you're not as fearless as you'd like me to believe. Are you?"

"W-why do you say that?"

Nick lowered his eyes to the base of her throat. "This," he pressed his finger on her pounding pulse, "gives you away."

A slight blush rose up her cheeks. She tightened the towel and edged back again, losing her balance. Nick reached an arm around her waist, pulling her forward. She landed against his chest. Her eyes widened as she sucked in a breath.

Nick had the sudden urge to keep her pressed against him, which both confused and irritated him. He pulled her away from the edge of the pool, and then stepped back to put some distance between them. "You should be more careful."

"You put me in the position to fall."

"You put yourself in a position to fall. You should never have gone to the cottage, Cali. It wasn't a smart move."

"Oh, yeah? What if I told you I found something that may help us find her?"

"What?"

"I found a ticket stub. I think she went to the Coral Isle Lighthouse last Wednesday. And she wasn't alone."

"You think so?"

"Yes. It was a ticket for two admissions."

"I know."

Her brows lifted. "You do?" she asked in a high-pitched voice.

"Yes. She went with a neighbor who had rented a cottage next door to her."

"Did you interrogate this neighbor?"

"Well," Nick rubbed his hand across the scratchy stubble on his jaw, "I didn't exactly handcuff the elderly woman and haul her to the station, but I did ask her questions."

"Elderly woman?" The hope in Cali's eyes

dwindled, and he felt a twinge of regret.

"Yes, elderly. She and Serena went to visit the lighthouse together. It was no big deal." He tilted his head and lowered his voice, "Cali, I know you think you're helping, but the man who took her is dangerous. You need to stop snooping around before you get hurt."

"Tell me what you know about him."

"I know you don't want to cross paths with him."

"That's original." Cali flipped her long hair behind her shoulders and began tapping her right foot again. "Why don't you tell me something I don't know?"

Nick clenched his hands into fists and crossed his arms. Shaking his head, he said, "You have no idea what this man is capable of."

"If you tell me, then I'd know wouldn't I?"

He ground his teeth and sighed as his irritation grew. "It's getting late. I'll walk you back to your room." He turned on his heel and picked up the water bottles, napkin and the sandwich wrapper, dumping them into the poolside trash can before facing her again.

"So that's it? You won't tell me anything?"

"No. I *can't* tell you anything. Not yet."

Cali looked away, took in a deep breath and walked past him out of the pool gate. He let her lead the way back to her rented room. Stopping in front of the door, she wrapped her arms around herself and studied her toes.

Nick slipped the key into the slot and turned it, opening the door an inch. When she moved to step inside, he caught her slender arm in his grasp. "Stop snooping, Cali. Don't put yourself at risk."

Her full lips tightened. "I can take care of myself."

"Yeah? That's probably what Serena thought, too."

A brief flash of pain crossed her eyes before they

became guarded.

"Listen Cali, I'm only trying to keep you safe. It's my duty to protect you."

Renewed determination swirled in her eyes along with a spark of anger. "Yeah? Well, don't do me any favors. It was your duty to protect Serena too. And look what happened to her."

Chapter Four

Guilt injected itself into Cali's thoughts, winding its way through her system to the point where she picked up her cell phone the next morning to call the sheriff and apologize. Her words spoken in anger last night had been unfair. It was not his fault Serena was missing, but Cali needed an outlet for her anger and frustration, and Nick Justice was a good target. Now, after a restless night of sleep, her conscience prodded her into punching in the numbers to the sheriff's office, but she quickly snapped her cell phone shut before the first ring finished.

With a heavy groan, Cali grabbed her purse and headed out the door, knowing a sincere apology sounded better when given face to face. An unexpected sense of anticipation in seeing Sheriff Justice again sent her pulse into overdrive before even making it to her car.

Considering ways to apologize as she drove a few miles north on the beach road, she decided a long drawn out apology was uncalled for and settled for a quick, *Sorry about what I said last night.* Why she had to rehearse it in her head several times, she could not figure out. How hard could it be to say she was sorry? And why did her pulse rate increase as she approached the office?

By the time she pulled into the parking lot, her nerves had unraveled, and she almost turned around. Almost. The only thing keeping her from leaving was the fact that she had spent over two hours the night before, after Sheriff Justice left the motel, writing detailed notes about Serena that she thought might be helpful in the investigation. She only hoped Sheriff Justice had been serious when he said he would take the time to read them.

She pulled three pages of notes out of her purse and headed inside the office, trying to ignore the overwhelming humidity that greeted her every time she set foot outside.

A deputy she hadn't seen before opened the door to leave the office as she approached. The nearly bald, stocky man tipped his head in greeting and held the door open.

"Thanks." She walked in and found the entire office empty, except for the dispatcher, who looked up from her desk with a warm smile.

"Morning."

"Hello, I'm..."

"Ms. Stevens. I remember you," the woman said with a relaxed country drawl. "I didn't get a chance to introduce myself yesterday because we were so busy. The full moon seems to rile people up something awful. Anyway, I'm so sorry about your friend being missing and all." She held out a hand full of plump fingers. "I'm Helen H."

"Helen H.?" Cali tilted her head slightly, and shook the offered hand. She expected a gentle grip, but the woman surprised her with a firm shake.

"Yes. The H. stands for Huckleberry. But, I got tired of being razzed about my name. I put up with the jokes for too long, ever since way back in fifth grade. I finally got fed up with it and then...well, I've been telling people to call me Ms. H. for years now. But, feel free to call me Helen," she said with a mixture of humor and warmth in her voice.

"All right, Helen," Cali agreed, returning the smile.

The phone rang and Helen held up a finger. "Just a minute."

Cali turned to give her privacy and looked around the waiting area. Two doors to the left led to offices. One office was the sheriff's; she didn't know who claimed the other one. To the right of Helen's desk, an open door led to a long hallway. Cali took a step to the side to peek down the passageway, and several sets of steel bars came into view. She gave an involuntary shudder. Thinking about being trapped inside one of those cells roused her dormant claustrophobia and made her back away until the cells were no longer in sight.

"Don't worry, Ms. Stevens. The sheriff's not likely to lock you up in one of them cells. Unless you break a law or two, of course." Helen hung up the phone and leaned her elbows on the tall front desk. She nudged a plate of coffee cake toward Cali. "You look like you haven't eaten much lately. Please, have a slice."

Cali was about to decline, but the hopeful look on the woman's face changed her mind. She picked up a piece and took a bite. The cinnamon sugar melted in her mouth. "This is delicious."

"Thanks. Sometimes I get the notion to bake, and I'll bring in something for my boys now and then."

"Your boys?"

Affection filled Helen's smile. "Yeah. The sheriff and his deputies. Of course, you've met the sheriff and talked with Deputy Owen. The one you passed by on your way in was Deputy Castle. All together, there are seven of them. Course, you won't see them all here during the day, seeing how they work different shifts."

Cali would hardly call Sheriff Justice or Deputy Castle boys, but she kept her opinion to herself. She finished the small slice of coffee cake and dusted the crumbs from her fingers. "Speaking of the sheriff. Is he here? I have something to give him."

"No. Sorry. He's out on a call. But I'll be happy to give it to him for you." She extended a hand toward the papers Cali held.

Disappointment rushed through her. "You can give him these." She handed the detailed notes to Helen. "But you can't give him the other thing I came here to give him."

Helen's weathered-green eyes sparkled as her lips turned up into a mischievous grin. "And just what would that be?"

Cali felt a blush rise at how her statement must have sounded. "An apology."

"Ahh." Helen's grin faded into a serious expression. "Well, I don't know what you're sorry about, but if you have an apology to make, I admire you for wanting to tell him in person. But, you'll have to wait. You see, the call he's out on might take a while. When Old Man Kingsley takes a notion to get riled up about something, he takes some time getting cooled down. And Sheriff Justice is the only one who can do the calming. He has a certain finesse about him, you know."

Helen folded the papers Cali had given her and stuffed them into a white envelope. She scribbled something on the front before licking the envelope closed. "Seems this time the old man's gotten himself all upset about the new speed bump they installed down at the old general store. And when he gets upset, he pulls out his shotgun and lets everyone in his neighborhood know about it." Helen shook her head, her fluffy, gray hair bouncing lightly. "I tell you, if it ain't one thing it's another."

The thought of an irate man waving a shotgun at Sheriff Justice made Cali's heart skid, and she swallowed. "I suppose the sheriff's used to handling situations like that...right?"

"Oh, yeah." Helen waved absently. "Nick's been through much worse situations before. He can handle it. Don't worry. He'll be back to look for your missing friend."

"Oh, I didn't mean..." Cali took a deep breath and let it out. "I just...I'd hate to see anything happen to him."

"Ahh. I see." The woman's grin returned in full force.

Cali cleared her throat and edged toward the door. "I mean...well, you know. I'd hate to see any officer hurt in the line of duty. Or off duty. Or anytime." She wondered what kind of fool Helen must think of her now. Deciding she had done enough damage, she said, "I'd better get going. Thanks for breakfast."

"Sure thing. Oh, and Ms. Stevens..."

"Call me Cali."

"OK Cali. Nick's a good man. Honest. Trustworthy. You can rely on him to do what's necessary to find your friend."

"That's good to know. Thanks." She stepped outside and slid on her sunglasses, wondering if she would ever be able to have as much faith in the sheriff as Helen did.

Chapter Five

Cali had every intention of driving to various tourist attractions and asking if anyone had remembered seeing Serena. The Coral Isle Aquarium made the top of her list, considering how Serena had always had a fascination with marine life. But, as Cali drove along the main road, a red flag on the beach caught her eye. She recognized it as a warning that no swimming was allowed, probably due to a strong rip current. It gave her an idea, and she made a U-turn at the next light, heading straight back to the cottage that Sheriff Justice had warned her to stay clear of last night.

Her heart pounded as she pulled into an open parking spot next to the cottage. She scolded herself for letting the sheriff's warning intimidate her. He was not willing to share his evidence with her, so what was she supposed to do? Sit back and do nothing? Not a chance.

Cali pulled her hair back into a haphazard ponytail, stuffed a picture of Serena into her pocket and stepped out. The sweltering heat hit her again, making her glad she had chosen to wear a tank top along with a pair of lightweight shorts. She locked her car, pocketed the keys and headed for the beach.

A breeze collided with her at the top of the

protective sand dunes, cooling her already damp skin. To the left, she spotted five lifeguard stands spaced out evenly along the beach before a long fishing pier cut off the view. To the right, another four stands lined the beach. Each had a red flag posted nearby. The ocean did not look ominous to her, but Cali assumed the lifeguards must consider the undertow to be at a dangerous level.

She removed her flip-flops, picked them up and headed to the first lifeguard stand. *Lord, please let somebody remember seeing Serena.*

"Hello," Cali called out as she approached the lifeguard perched on the stand. A splatter of pimples adorned the young woman's face, and Cali guessed her to be no older than a teenager. She wore her dark hair pulled back into a bun at the nape of her neck, a one-piece solid red swimsuit and a whistle around her neck, which made her appear confident and official despite her young age. Cali wondered how much experience a teenager could possibly have, and how much help the girl would turn out to be.

The lifeguard straightened, looking at Cali with wide, curious brown eyes. "Is something wrong?" She scanned the ocean as she stood, and picked up a rescue buoy, ready to take action.

"No." Cali redirected the anxious lifeguard's attention. "I'm just looking for a friend." She pulled the picture of Serena out of her pocket and handed it to the girl.

"Oh." Her features relaxed. She waved the picture around without looking at it. "This is my second day out here alone. Until yesterday, I've been in training. I'd sure hate to run into a problem this soon."

"What's your name?"

"Anna."

"Anna, I'm Cali Stevens. My friend..." she indicated the picture.

"Oh, yes." Anna blushed and giggled. "Sorry." She looked at the picture. "I haven't noticed her out here today. What's she wearing?"

"She's been missing since Friday. I don't know what she was wearing, or even when she was out here." Cali's hopes deflated. How could she expect to find help without even having the basic details? "She rented a nearby cottage last week, and I'm sure she came out to the beach at least a few times."

"Oh, I'm sorry; I can't help you. All last week I was stationed with Chad. We were only in this area for a day or two, but mostly we were down at number nine."

"Number nine?" Cali peered across the length of the beach.

"Yeah. It's the stand way down there. The last one you can see." She pointed to the right. "Chad's a full-timer. He even has the power to arrest people, and get this...he was my mentor for all of last month." Anna's slight blush deepened. "He's totally cool."

Cali wondered if Anna had a crush on her 'totally cool' mentor. "So you're not assigned to the same place each day you work?"

Anna shook her head. "Nope. We rotate shifts on each of the nine stands. That way we don't get bored."

Cali didn't understand how changing stands could possible affect boredom levels. The sand, tourists and ocean all looked the same no matter which stretch of the beach she looked at.

Anna must have seen her confusion. "It's not the same." She pointed to the left. "See over there. From that station, we have to keep an eye on a sandbar out about fifty yards. People go out there and think they can touch bottom, then a wave comes and they can't touch anymore. Sometimes they panic. I've seen it happen for real." Anna pointed to the right. "See over there. The bottom drops out much quicker than over here, where I'm responsible for. This is the easiest station. I guess that's why Chad put me here first." She shrugged and scanned the ocean again.

"I didn't realize how involved it all is. Your parents must be proud." Cali hoped to boost the girl's ego, in order to get as much information from her as possible.

Anna turned to her and beamed. "They are kinda proud."

A radio resting on the lifeguard stand crackled, and Anna reached for it. A woman's voice spoke over the line, "Better watch the waves kiddo. You don't want to get caught not paying attention." Anna jumped and set down the radio as if it had burned her to touch it. She looked to the left.

The lifeguard in the next stand was watching them with her arms crossed. Cali assumed the older woman must be assigned to look out for the new kid and keep her in line.

"Sorry. Didn't mean to get you in trouble. I'll get going."

Anna didn't pry her eyes from the ocean as she said, "Sorry I couldn't help you."

"I need Serena's picture back."

Anna sneaked a peek at the picture again. "I'll keep looking out for her. If I see her how do I reach you?"

"If you see her, call the sheriff's office." Cali took the picture from the girl and slid it into her pocket. "Thanks." She headed to the next stand to the right, intentionally avoiding the temperamental lifeguard who'd caught her talking to Anna.

She wove her way around dozens of tourists who appeared to be enjoying the sun and sand, and cautiously approached the next lifeguard, hoping to find a more experienced person guarding this area of the beach. When she walked to the stand, she found a red-headed young man, guessing him to be in his late teens or early twenties.

"Afternoon, ma'am. May I help you?" he asked as he rubbed a handful of lotion on his freckled arms.

"I hope so."

The young man sat forward with a smile. "I hope so, too."

His words sounded sincere, and Cali's hopes raised a notch. "I'm Cali Stevens and I'm looking for my friend, Serena Taylor. She may have been out here a few times last week. Have you seen her?" She produced the picture.

He stood and jumped from the stand, stretching as if he had been immobile for a few hours. "I'm Trey." He nodded a greeting. "Let me take a look at her."

As he moved closer, Cali caught the scent of the sun block he was applying. It didn't have the typical coconut aroma. Instead, it held the strong, fruity scent of limes.

"What's her name again?" he asked as he leaned over the picture and continued rubbing the lotion in.

"Serena."

"I'm pretty good at remembering faces, but I don't remember seeing her around here lately. Why are you looking for her?"

"I haven't been able to get in touch with her since last Friday."

Trey glanced toward the ocean, then cupped his hands around his mouth and yelled, "Hey buddy! No swimming."

Cali turned in time to see a tall, lanky man starting to wade into the water. He stopped and turned, but did not come out. He appeared to be trying to decide if he would listen to Trey's warning or not.

Trey glanced at his watch. "I'll give him thirty seconds." He crossed his arms and continued to watch the would-be swimmer.

"What happens if he doesn't listen to you?"

"I make him listen," he said in a serious tone.

Cali hesitated at the authority in Trey's voice. Apparently, he took his job seriously. She waited a moment before asking, "Why are the no swimming flags posted anyway?"

"There's a tropical storm brewing off the coast, causing strong rip currents. The storm's stagnant right now. But, they say it may turn into a hurricane and head this way," Trey said as he continued to watch the stubborn man standing in the water. "You never know which direction the storms will end up going."

After several glances to the lifeguard, the man stepped out of the water, but remained standing close to the edge.

"I thought so," Trey mumbled as he visibly relaxed.

"I didn't know there was even a possibility of a hurricane coming."

"It's still off a ways. Too early to tell."

Assuming Trey had no useful information about Serena, she started to step away. "Well, I don't want to interrupt your job, so I'll get going."

Before he could respond, the sound of a vehicle approaching caught their attention. Trey held up a hand in greeting and stepped toward an all terrain vehicle as it slowed to a stop. The driver of the ATV looked to be in his mid-twenties, and his red swim trunks and black whistle indicated his position as a lifeguard. His tangled, sun-bleached blonde hair contrasted with his deep, bronzed tan. His appearance reminded Cali of the cross between a beach bum and a surfer.

"Hey Trey, are you using up all of my lotion? When are you going to start remembering to bring your own?" he asked when Trey rubbed on a little more lotion.

"Probably never," he said with a sheepish grin.

"Hello." The man got off the vehicle and

approached Cali. "I'm Chad." He held out a hand in greeting.

"Cali." She offered her hand. His grip was firm, but his skin felt softer than she anticipated on a man who obviously spent much time outside.

He tilted his head to the side. "Are you distracting another one of my lifeguards?"

She tensed.

His smile showed a set of even white teeth. "Don't worry. When I put Shelly in charge of watching over Anna, she decided to take her job a little too seriously."

Trey asked, "Is Shelly tattle-tailing again?"

"Yep." Chad looked at Cali, but a slow smile grew on his face. "Don't worry; I'm not as strict as they'd have you believe. So, what's going on?" He lifted an arm and leaned against Trey's lifeguard stand.

"Are you in charge out here? The leader..." Cali felt warmth crawl up her already heated skin. "I mean the head lifeguard?"

Chad lifted his sunglasses and secured them on his head. "Something like that, yeah." His bright, teasing grin returned, and his green eyes sparkled.

No wonder Anna has a crush on him. He probably has all the teenaged girls drooling over him. "I'm looking for my friend." She held out Serena's picture. "Have you seen her?"

Chad stepped closer, the same lime scent radiated around him. He started to take the picture, but stopped when Trey yelled again, this time with the help of a bullhorn.

"Get out of the water now!" Trey glanced at Chad and added, "Sir."

The lanky fellow, who'd had a hard time following Trey's orders, was now swimming out into the ocean.

"I said no swimming!" Trey's agitation showed through his voice.

"I've got it," Chad said, grabbing the red buoy and removing his sunglasses. He took off in a sprint to the water, drawing many curious gazes. A few minutes later, he came out, dragging the stubborn, sputtering man alongside him.

They exchanged a few heated words before the man packed his belongings and left the beach. Chad ambled back, swiping the remaining water droplets from his face. He headed straight for Cali. "If there's one thing I won't tolerate, it's people not doing what we tell them to do. Now, about this friend of yours."

"Oh, yes." The smell of salty ocean water now mixed with his fruity lotion scent. Uncomfortable at how close he stood, she held the picture out and stepped back at the same time, hoping he wouldn't notice her retreat.

"I don't recognize her, but I can show this picture around if you'd like." Chad started to take the picture.

She pulled it back and tucked it into her pocket. "I only have the one copy." She felt renewed heat consume her cheeks. "I know I should've made extras to leave with people, but I came here in a hurry. I'm desperate to find her."

Chad appeared to consider her words. "I can give you a ride to each of my stands." He walked to the ATV and sat on it. The water from his wet swimsuit pooled on the black vinyl seat. He patted the area behind him. "We can see if anyone in my team has seen her."

Hopping on an ATV and riding behind Chad may have appealed to someone like Anna, but Cali had no intentions of putting her arms around, and holding onto, a stranger's muscular abs. "I appreciate it, but I'd rather walk." She took a breath and added, "It's good exercise."

Chad watched her carefully. Instead of insisting, he said, "Good luck to you then." He started the ATV and nodded at her, then at Trey before continuing along the beach.

She turned to Trey, who had positioned himself back onto his assigned post. "Thanks anyway. It was nice to meet you."

The young redhead nodded. "You too, Cali. I hope you find her."

"So do I," she said, but her hopes had already begun to diminish, and her level of frustration multiplied.

The day grew warmer with each passing minute, and Cali wondered how long she would be able to tolerate the high temperatures as she trudged along the beach. She slipped her flip-flops back on, trying to avoid the sting of the burning sand.

Doubts flooded her mind, and Cali wondered if she had wasted her time. *What are the chances a lifeguard who sees hundreds of people every day would remember Serena anyway?*

She stopped, closed her eyes and took a moment to pray. *Lord, lead me to the right place...please! I haven't had any luck yet, and I need direction from You. What do I do? Where do I go?*

She opened her eyes and looked around. The only thing she noticed, that she hadn't before, was a set of hungry seagulls circling overhead, and a group of sandpipers greedily poking their beaks into the sand in search of food. She sighed. "What did you expect? A huge sign pointing from the sky saying 'look here Cali'?"

She stepped around an older couple who sat close together, sharing a large beach towel. The woman spoke up, "You know the heat's getting to you when you start talking to yourself. Maybe you ought to head inside and get a drink before you start hallucinating, too." The woman's tender, grandmotherly smile reminded Cali of her own grandmother.

Cali laughed. "I guess I should." She hesitated. "Inside where?"

The woman pointed to the right. "Over there. Past that dune."

Looking closely, Cali's heart raced. *Thank you, Lord.* She had found her next destination.

Chapter Six

The sight of the well-populated, quaint beachfront restaurant restored Cali's hope. A large teal and white striped canvas awning provided a barrier to the midday sun, while an array of decorative aluminum patio tables and chairs invited beachgoers to walk up in their swimsuits and sandals to enjoy a casual meal. Cali stepped into the shade, instantly relieved to be out of the direct sunlight. She felt a slight breeze coming from several ceiling fans spinning in lazy circles overhead.

She removed her sunglasses and noticed a handwritten sign that read, 'please seat yourself.' She scanned the outdoor tables and found every one of them full. Her latent appetite awakened and hit full force as her gaze landed on a set of young men. A large, oval plate full of French fries topped with layers of melted cheddar cheese and crumbles of real bacon sat between them, and the smell of the salty fries and freshly cooked bacon made her mouth water. Her empty stomach tactfully reminded her it was time to eat. Forcing her gaze from the sinful sight, she immediately witnessed another.

A tray filled with a wide assortment of foods ranging from fried onion rings and grilled hamburgers to tossed salads and colorful side vegetables sat behind her, ready to be distributed.

Cali caught her gaze scanning the tray and forced her focus away from the tempting plates. With nothing more than her keys and Serena's picture in her pockets, she considered turning around and heading back to her car to retrieve some money for lunch. After a moment, she decided she could wait for food; finding a lead to Serena's location was much more important.

She passed through the patio and walked inside the restaurant. Standing in the doorway, she let her eyes adjust to the inside lighting. Scanning the interior of the restaurant, her hopes of speaking to the staff diminished as she caught sight of how they scrambled to keep up with customers' orders. Her only hope in grabbing their attention was to find a table and wait for one of them to come to her.

Cali searched the room, and her gaze landed on several conversation-filled customers as they dined and enjoyed their meals. Then her gaze caught on a familiar face and stopped in mid-scan. Sheriff Justice sat at a corner table, his deep-blue eyes already locked onto her. Her heart lurched into high gear, as if it had an agenda of its own, and she sucked in a deep breath forcing herself not to look away. Considering his profession, he had probably been aware of her presence since the moment she stepped through the door. Most lawmen were keen observers, and it was obvious that Sheriff Justice was no exception.

A deputy sitting across the table from the sheriff turned to see what had captured his boss's attention. With both sets of eyes on her, Cali felt self-conscious, as she stood immobile in the doorway of the hectic restaurant.

Sheriff Justice lifted his head a notch to acknowledge her, and then waved her toward his table. She wanted to ignore his gesture, to ignore his presence altogether. But, considering every other table was occupied, and she still owed him an apology, her conscience prodded her forward, one leaden step at a time.

As she neared the table, Sheriff Justice stood and pulled out a chair. Her face warmed at the thoughtful gesture, which made her feel even more like her statement the previous night had been out of line. She took the offered seat and settled into it as he returned to his chair.

"This is Deputy Owen," Sheriff Justice indicated the officer sitting to her left.

She turned to greet the deputy and shook the hand he offered. Arrogance showed through the flashy smile he produced. His palm felt cool against her heated skin, and his gentle grip lingered as he said, "It's nice to meet you in person." His smile temporarily widened his long, narrow face as his gaze darted to the front of her yellow tank top then back to her eyes.

Cali recognized his voice as the one she had spoken to over the phone about Serena's disappearance. He sounded pleasant enough over the phone, but something about him in person made her uneasy. She pulled her hand away, wary of the unusually long greeting.

She glanced at Sheriff Justice. A crease formed across his forehead and his jaw tightened. He leaned forward in his seat. "You need to get back to the station, Deputy."

"But we haven't ordered..."

Sheriff Justice's pointed look silenced the man's protest. Deputy Owen retrieved his hat from where it rested on the table. "I'll go and see if any new information has come in regarding Ms. Taylor's case." He looked at Cali. "Don't worry ma'am. We'll find her." He took one more glance at the sheriff, stood and strutted away.

"You didn't have to make him leave," Cali said, but felt a sense of relief that he had.

"His pride will recover." He held out a menu.

Cali shook her head. "I'm not staying for lunch."

A challenge sparked in his eyes as he set the menu in front of her. "If you didn't come here for lunch, then why are you here?"

She swallowed a lump forming in her throat. He would not like the truth, but she found it impossible to skirt around. "I came to find answers."

Sheriff Justice leaned closer, crossing his arms and placing them on the table. "I told you to stay out of this investigation." His determination showed through his unwavering blue-eyed censure.

"I know." Cali began to feel trapped. She set her jaw, shrugged her shoulders and defended herself. "But, someone has to do something."

A corner of his mouth lifted. "Your confidence in my abilities is overwhelming."

Taken aback at his direct appraisal, she said, "Look. I'm only being honest. I think you could be doing more to find her."

"More?"

"Yes, more. How much time are you wasting here having lunch when you could be out looking for her?"

"I'm not wasting time by being here."

A young, bleached-blonde waitress appeared at the table. Her mouth turned into a syrupy smile as her focus landed on the sheriff. She set a glass of water in front of him. "What can I do for you, Sheriff? I mean...get for you?" she purred sweetly.

Good grief. Cali held back a sigh. The way the twenty-something woman fawned over him instantly annoyed her. She couldn't pinpoint why it bothered her, but it did. She recognized the sheriff's appeal, but the way the girl flirted with him was nauseating.

He acknowledged the waitress then looked directly at Cali. Nodding his head he said, "Ladies first."

Cali shook her head and slid her chair back preparing to leave, knowing she didn't have a way to pay for her meal. Sheriff Justice placed his large, warm hand on her forearm to keep her from leaving. "It's my treat. Order what you'd like."

Finding no way to make a graceful exit without causing a scene, she relented. "All right." She pulled her chair back to the table and glanced at the daily specials on the menu. She looked at the waitress, who eyed her sullenly. "I'll take the chicken salad croissant sandwich with fries."

Sheriff Justice ordered a turkey club sandwich with fries, and the woman turned to leave, swinging her hips side to side a little more than necessary. Cali turned back to meet the sheriff's tight expression. A small part of her was glad he had completely ignored the waitress's attempts to gain his attention.

He leaned back and clasped his hands in front of him. "So if I'm wasting my time here, aren't you wasting yours, too?"

"No. I came here for something more than food."

He quirked an eyebrow.

"I wanted to find out if anyone who works here has seen Serena. Since this place is so close to the cottage she rented, I have a feeling she might have come here a time or two. Maybe she came here with someone. Maybe with a man. I have so many questions..."

"Speaking of questions, I have one for you. How many times did you talk to Serena while she was on vacation?"

Cali felt a pang of guilt. "Once. And only for a few minutes. I had a deadline on an article. I should've taken the time to talk longer."

"Did she mention meeting anyone?"

She sighed heavily. "You know she didn't. It's in the report. Deputy Owen already asked me."

"I know he did. But sometimes when I ask someone a question, they don't have a complete, detailed answer until they've had time to think it over."

Cali knew that to be true from her experience as a reporter. "That's why I always give people I interview my card. They often call me later with details they've forgotten."

"So you see why I asked."

"Yes, I do."

The waitress appeared and refilled Sheriff Justice's glass of water. *Funny how she didn't bother to ask me what I wanted to drink.* Sheriff Justice must have noticed too, because he spoke up and asked the waitress to bring another glass of water.

Once again, startled by his thoughtfulness, Cali felt heat climb her cheeks. She still needed to apologize, but wasn't quite ready to do it. Looking for a distraction, she caught the waitress's attention and read the name on her tag. "Jillian." Cali lifted Serena's picture from her pocket. "Have you seen this woman before?"

Jillian's big, brown eyes darted to the picture briefly. Looking back at Cali she said, "Yeah."

Cali sat straighter as her heart leapt into overdrive. She gave the young woman her full attention. "When?"

"When the sheriff showed me her picture yesterday. And when he showed me her picture again today."

Cali parted her lips, but the questions she had formed in her mind lodged in her throat, leaving her mouth hanging wide.

Apparently, the waitress enjoyed seeing her squirm because she scoffed, "What's the matter? Did the law man beat you to the investigation?" Jillian turned on her heel and sashayed away again. With wide eyes, Cali turned to meet the sheriff's unreadable expression.

He leaned forward. "Did you really think I was only here for lunch? I want to find Ms. Taylor...Serena as much as you do."

Embarrassed beyond reason, Cali found it hard to look him in the eye. She looked at the table, discovering a tiny breadcrumb on the tablecloth. She swiped it away, giving herself a moment to recover. He lifted his glass of water and took a long swallow before setting it back on the table. Her gaze followed his thumb as it caressed the condensation from the crystal-clear glass he still held. A bolt of awareness shot through her, making it difficult to remain focused on the words of apology she had formulated. Gathering her courage, she began to speak, but the waitress intervened when she returned with their food.

After setting their plates on the table, Jillian turned her back on Cali. "Is there anything else I can get for you Sheriff?"

Cali resisted the urge to roll her eyes.

"Not for me. Cali?"

"I'd like a bottle of ketchup, please."

Jillian walked away without a word.

Cali took a bite of her fries then reached for the salt. "Do you come here often?"

"Not usually. Why?"

"The waitress seems to be rather fond of you."

A deep chuckle rumbled from his chest and a striking smile landed on his face. "I've been in here a few times recently, and she's been my waitress more than once. She's never acted like this before, but this is the first time I've been here with a woman. I think she's jealous."

Cali wasn't sure why that statement sent a spiral of satisfaction through her veins, but it did. Looking for a diversion from the unexpected emotion, she took a bite of her croissant. After swallowing she asked, "So, how did things turn out with Old Man Kingsley?"

His eyebrows lifted. "How do you know…? Oh, Helen," he answered his own question as if he should have known to begin with. "It wasn't so bad. This time I didn't even have to arrest him."

"Did he shoot at you?"

"No. He's mostly talk." He ate a French fry before taking a bite of his thick, layered sandwich.

"Mostly? How did you calm him down?"

"I gave him what he wants."

"You're removing the speed bump?"

He grinned. "No. He just wants someone to listen to him. Really listen."

"That's all?"

"When he gets upset about something, he spouts off about his latest annoyance, and I listen. By time he's done talking, he's burned his own aggression out. I usually don't have to do anything else."

"You must have a lot of patience." She lifted her napkin and patted her lips.

His gaze followed her motions. "It takes a lot of patience to do what I do."

"I imagine it does."

Cali had barely eaten a third of her sandwich before Sheriff Justice finished his and dug into his fries. Between bites he commented, "Brookstone isn't too far from here. I'm surprised you haven't come here on vacation before."

"How do you know I haven't?"

"Your dad told me."

Cali choked on the food in her mouth. She looked for a glass, but since Jillian had conveniently forgotten her drink, she had nothing to help ease her spats of coughing.

"Take mine." He scooted his glass over.

She hesitated for a fraction of a second before taking several sips of water. When her coughing eased she asked, "My dad told you? When?"

Finished with his fries, he set the napkin on his plate and set it aside. "When I called him this morning."

"You called my father? Why?"

He shrugged. "I was hoping to talk him into

bringing you home to Brookstone."

She straightened, and her muscles tensed. "And?"

"And, he says he's always encouraged you to make your own decisions and stick by them."

Grateful for the support, her tension eased, and she beamed. "That's my dad."

His expression turned serious. "Even though he also wishes you would come home."

Her smile faltered. "You both can forget it. I'm not leaving."

He started to say something when Jillian magically appeared with the bill. "I hope everything was all right." She set a bottle of ketchup in front of Cali and then immediately took both plates from the table.

"You have impeccable timing." The words slipped from Cali's lips before she could filter them.

"I've been told that before." Jillian turned her syrupy smile on Cali.

"I'll bet."

Sheriff Justice gave a loud cough. "Thank you, Jillian."

The woman stepped to him and set a hand on his shoulder. "You're more than welcome. I'm just sorry none of us here could help you find any of the women that have gone missing." She shrugged her shoulders. "At least the others showed up eventually. This one probably will, too."

His gaze shot to Cali a second after the waitress spoke the words.

She stared at him. *Any of the women?*

Chapter Seven

Nick handed Jillian enough cash to cover the bill as Cali scooted her chair back and rushed toward the exit. He didn't include a tip. "Next time, try being a little bit nicer to my companion." He strode after Cali, ignoring the undignified words coming from Jillian's mouth.

He easily caught up. "Don't walk away from me."

"If I don't, I may end up saying something I'll regret later. Or...saying something I won't regret." She continued to weave her way out of the restaurant, stepping around a few customers. She slammed her sunglasses onto her face, and stalked out of the protective covering of the awning.

"You sure do rile easily."

Cali stopped and turned to face him. He stopped and stood at the edge of the patio decking waiting for her reply.

"I rile easily?" She stepped close with her head held high. "You should've told me about the other women."

A sharp gasp erupted, and Nick glanced at a middle-aged woman sitting at a nearby patio table. He assumed she had overheard Cali's last statement judging from the disapproving look she directed at him.

He ignored her.

"I would've thought you'd have figured it out on your own by now...seeing as how you are such an excellent investigative reporter and all."

Another, louder gasp sounded beside him. This time he didn't bother to acknowledge the disgruntled eavesdropper.

Color enflamed Cali's cheeks, and a muscle worked in her jaw before she turned, stalking across the hot sand toward the pounding ocean surf.

"You must be exhausted," he called out.

She stopped again and whirled around. Fury mixed with confusion in her eyes. He stood, balancing on one leg at a time as he ripped his shoes and socks off his feet, rolled up his pants legs and walked over.

The wind swept a tendril of hair across her cheek, and she jerked it aside as she waited. "What are you talking about?" She posted her hands on her hips.

Nick caught up with her in a few long strides. He shook his head slightly. "You must be exhausted," he repeated, "from carrying such a heavy load on your shoulders."

She creased her brow and turned, heading toward the water. He easily kept up with her fast, angry strides. After a moment, she had to make the decision to either stop or walk straight into the ocean. Although probably tempted to see how far he was willing to follow her, she stopped as soon as her feet hit the edge of the water and turned toward him again.

She simply stared with her chin held high. Waiting. Watching. Her pulse pounded at the base of her throat as she took in deep, ragged breaths.

Nick swept his gaze over her. "You're not the one in charge. The sooner you learn that, the better off you'll be."

Her eyes narrowed and she fisted her hands at

her sides. "If I were in charge, I would care about the people on my island."

He tightened his jaw, looked away and drew in a deep breath, trying to reign in his rising temper. He ground out the words, "I wasn't talking about me."

"Will you stop talking in cryptic circles? Spell it out if you have to. What are you trying to say?"

He twisted to the side and threw his shoes and socks on the dry sand. When he turned back, he placed his hands on her shoulders, firm enough to keep her facing him, yet gentle enough to keep from hurting her. "I'm talking about God. He is in charge. Not you. Not me."

The breath left her lungs in a rush. She shook her head. "I-I thought…"

His voice softened. "I know what my responsibilities are Cali. I also know my limitations. You don't seem to have discovered yours yet."

A large wave crashed along the shoreline, soaking the edges of Nick's rolled up pants as it bubbled and churned its way along the sand. He released her shoulders. She swayed. He didn't know if it was from the pull of the water as it receded back into the ocean, the relentless heat bearing down on her from the sun, or from the truth in the words he had spoken. He put a steadying arm around her waist and pulled her close, keeping her from falling into the rising tide.

His breath caught at the strong sensation of having her pressed against his side, and he fought to keep his mind where it should be.

Let her go.

Yet, his arm remained where it was, wrapped around her waist. She thrust away and stepped back, effectively helping him with his internal struggle. A myriad of emotions crossed her features.

He considered showing her the jagged scar on his left shoulder that provided a constant, aching reminder of his limitations. But, aside from stripping off his uniformed shirt and Kevlar vest in front of several tourists, he had no convenient way of showing her what had happened the night he had thought he could handle any situation alone.

"I understand you want to do everything you can to help find Serena. But, you're trying to carry a load which isn't yours to carry."

"Yeah? And you're trying to change the subject."

Another errant wave crashed into them, causing her to stumble again. He started to reach for her, but stopped when she put up her hands in defense.

"Don't."

"Cali, I…"

"How many?"

"What?"

"How many women have been abducted?"

He hesitated only a moment. "Serena's the third."

"What happened to the other two?"

Nick had to be careful. He could not give out any more information than could already be found in the local newspapers. "They've been found." The heat shimmering in her gaze turn into ice-cold fear. "Alive," he added quickly.

Cali let out a sigh and some of the fear in her gaze abated. "When? What happened to them? Who took them?"

Nick nodded politely at a young man walking past them carrying a long surfboard. A mother rounded up her squealing toddler, keeping her from running full-force into the crashing waves. He glanced to the area behind him. The tourists continued filling the beachfront, settling in for the afternoon with beach towels, umbrellas and chairs.

He looked back to Cali and held his hands up. "Not here."

"Why not here? Tell me. I have a right to know," she raised her voice, drawing attention from several other people.

Her demand snapped his carefully controlled patience. He stepped close, forcing her to retreat. "Do you? And what gives you that right? Just because you live a privileged life back home as daddy's little girl does not mean you have special privileges here on my island, and it does not give you the right to know the details of an ongoing investigation."

Cali backed away. She opened her mouth, and then clamped it shut without saying a word.

Nick turned, grabbed his shoes and socks, and walked away before the moisture gathering in Cali's eyes had a chance to breach his tight resolve, and make him feel more regrets than he already did.

Chapter Eight

"Dad?" Cali held her cell phone with shaky hands.

"Yes?"

"I want you to be honest with me."

"About what?"

"If I wasn't your daughter, would you have hired me as a reporter for the *Brookstone Herald*?"

"Why would you ask me something like that?"

"Because I need to know."

"You're good at your job, Cali. Don't ever doubt it."

"I don't doubt I'm good at it. But you have to admit, I wouldn't have been given the opportunity in the first place if you weren't my dad."

"Well, it is a family run business. That's how things work."

"Yes. But, I'd like to think I've earned my position at the Herald."

"You have earned it. What's all this about?"

"I don't know." She sighed and flopped back onto the bed in the motel room. Thankfully, the cleaning staff had changed the sheets on both mattresses today.

Bye-bye bed bugs.

She rubbed her forehead with her palm. "I think the heat's getting to me."

"Or maybe a certain officer of the law is getting to you?"

Cali sucked in a breath as her hand stilled. "How did you know?"

"I'm your dad remember? I can hear what you're not telling me. Even halfway across the state. What happened?"

"He thinks I'm pampered. He thinks I..." her voice trailed off. *He thinks I'm a daddy's girl.* Sheriff Justice's opinion shouldn't matter. But it did.

"Pampered? Is that what he said?"

"Not exactly. But he got me thinking about how much you and Mom have helped me out. With my job. With life. I just wonder where I'd be if I hadn't had so much support."

"So much support?" He let out a short laugh. "Honey, you've been the one supporting me for the last several years. Without you, this paper wouldn't sell half as well as it does. Did you know our circulation increased by thirteen percent this past quarter?"

"That's probably because Mrs. Welsby has stirred up trouble over the advice column. People are buying the paper to see what's gotten her hose tied in knots."

A raspy chuckle reverberated across the line. "Could be. But I think it has something to do with the new direction you've taken with your articles. We've had great feedback regarding the new human interest stories you've written in recent months."

"You always know how to make me feel better."

"I love you, hon'."

"I love you too, Dad." She took a breath, preparing to change the direction of the conversation. "I came across some new information today. Seems Serena's not the only one who's been abducted on Coral Isle recently."

"No kidding?"

"No kidding." Cali stood to pace the room as

anxiety filled her once again. "I went to the library and checked out past issues of the local paper. There's not much information, but I did find out two other women have been abducted recently. One in May, the other in July. One woman was in her mid-forties, the other was a teenager. They don't appear to be connected in any way, except they were both on the island alone."

"The teenaged girl was on the island alone?"

"She'd run away from home."

"I see."

"But listen to this. They both turned up after exactly two weeks."

"Turned up?"

"Yes. The abductor released them. The victims said they have very few memories of what happened. Drugs are suspected."

"What kind of drugs?"

"The paper didn't specify."

"They don't remember what happened to them?"

"I don't know. The paper was extremely vague. If I'd written the articles, they would've been much more detailed."

"I don't doubt it. Cali, maybe you should come back home. Let the sheriff handle it. It doesn't sound safe to be there."

She gritted her teeth and stopped pacing. Taking in a deep breath she said, "I have to find her."

"I knew you were gonna say that. Listen, your mom just came in. Want to say hi?"

Cali didn't have a chance to respond before her mother said, "I can't believe you didn't tell me you were leaving. What's going on with Serena?"

"I know I should've called. I'm sorry. About Serena? It's complicated. I'll let Dad fill you in on it." She didn't have the energy to go into the details with her mother, or to deal with her reaction when she found out about the abductions. Guilt nibbled at her for leaving her father with the arduous task, but it was not enough to make her change her mind.

"Oh, I'll never stop worrying about you. Are you eating enough? You don't sound like it. You know how worn down you get when you don't eat properly."

"Mom. I'm fine."

"Are you getting enough sleep?"

"Yes." Cali listened to her mother's worries and advice for a few more minutes before saying goodnight.

She flipped her phone closed and sank onto the bed, wondering if Sheriff Justice was right about her expectations. After living her whole life in a small town, around people who cared about her, maybe she did take certain things in life for granted.

Her thoughts strayed in multiple directions before she decided to flip on the television. Her mind needed a break as much as her body did. The mental stress had worn her down along with the hot, humid weather.

After discovering the remote control had been nailed to the end table sandwiched between the beds, it didn't take long to loop through the whole eight channels of reception on the TV. The only one that caught her interest was the local weather. A newscaster stood in front of a large map of the area, pinpointing the white, swirling storm threatening the East Coast. The forecaster made a general guess at when and where the storm could hit, but it was too early to be concerned about it. Right now, her focus had to remain on finding Serena.

She turned off the television and listened to the monotonous sound of the air-conditioning unit rattling in the window. As hard as she tried to unwind, her mind kept running in endless circles. Even with her father's reassurances, Sheriff Justice's words haunted her. Maybe his statement had more truth to it than she cared to admit.

Did she live her life expecting special privileges? She could see how the sheriff had formed his opinion, especially since she had walked into his office a stranger and demanded everything he knew about Serena's disappearance. Humility rose from somewhere deep inside, bringing with it another spurt of guilt.

Her tense muscles didn't relax until she prayed for guidance and for Serena's safe return. Snuggling deep under the covers, she didn't try to fight sleep. Although it was barely seven o'clock, she soon drifted off into a dreamless oblivion.

What seemed like minutes later, her cell phone rang.

She flipped it open without looking at the caller ID. "Hello?" Her voice sounded low and raspy.

"Did I wake you?"

She bolted upright. "Sheriff?" Hearing his clear, deep voice caused an unexpected wave of goose bumps to travel up her arms. Not the creepy kind of goose bumps. But the good kind. The kind that made her nerve endings feel alive. An odd sensation considering she was still mad, even if his earlier words did have a ring of truth.

"Yeah. It's me. Sorry to call so late."

Cali automatically glanced at the bedside clock before she wiggled back under the covers and cleared her throat. "Is it ten-thirty already?" The darkness outside the window agreed with the time on the clock. "I must've fallen asleep."

"I won't keep you. I just wanted to let you know I'm holding a press conference tomorrow afternoon regarding the abductions. It'll be on the local channels. You'll have some of the answers you've been waiting for."

Her heart pounded and she came fully awake. "So you do have more information?"

"A little. But not enough."

"Can you tell me now?"

Sheriff Justice hesitated and blew out a breath. "No."

"Why?" She had a feeling she already knew the answer. "Is it because I'm a reporter? You don't trust I'll keep it to myself?"

"We aren't the only two people involved in this. Too much is at stake. You'll have to wait until everyone else hears about it tomorrow."

Cali felt a tinge of disappointment. "What can you tell the public tomorrow you can't tell me now?"

He sighed. "Cali..."

Her newfound humility returned and she said, "Never mind. Forget I even asked. Sometimes I forget I'm not in my hometown, and you have no reason to trust me. You have no reason to treat me different from any other stranger on the street."

His voice softened, "I was out of line earlier today on the beach. I'm sorry."

Although she wanted to remain angry, the sincerity in his voice weakened her resolve. There hadn't been many men in her life willing to apologize without being forced into it, and she appreciated his offer.

Cali ran a hand through her tangled hair. "I'm sorry, too."

He lowered his voice close to a whisper, "And for the record, I don't think of you as a stranger." He disconnected, leaving her alone with his intimate words echoing in the lonely, old motel room.

Chapter Nine

Nick spent the entire morning preparing statements for the press and preparing for the many possible scenarios he may have to face in result of them. Going public with the information regarding Serena's disappearance, in connection with the other two abductions, was sure to create a feast for the reporters and at the least, major concern among the inhabitants of Coral Isle. It was also likely he would be dealing with more than a few panicked citizens. After all, Coral Isle was known for its beautiful beaches and family oriented attractions, not for its criminal activities.

As Nick prepared to leave his office, he said a quick prayer. *Lord, please help me get through to the women that may be his next targets. Please lead us to Serena, and keep her safe.*

Serena.

When had he begun to think of the missing woman by her first name? Was it the first time Cali entered his office, pleading for him to find her friend? Or, was it sometime after, as he learned more about Serena? He had read the notes Cali dropped off at the station yesterday. Nick didn't know if any of the information could be used to help find her, but it did show him the person behind the name.

Taking out his brief notes, he wrote the words *'make it personal.'* He wanted everyone listening to be concerned not only about their own safety, but to care about finding Serena. What better way to inspire people to help find Serena, than to make them care. An idea sparked, and he reached for his cell phone.

A brisk knock sounded, interrupting his racing thoughts. He opened it to find Deputy Owen with an excited look on his face, and his weight shifting from one foot to the next.

"They're all waiting for you, Sheriff. You should see the crowd. It's the biggest turnout I've ever seen for one of our press conferences. All of the major news channels are here. And guess what? There are a couple of guys from CNN out there. Can you believe it?" He smiled like a little boy on Christmas morning.

Irritation rocketed through Nick. "This isn't something to be happy about Owen," he snapped. "I spoke to Mayor Wilson an hour ago. And I have to return a phone call to the Governor. Apparently he's concerned about having a serial rapist on the loose in his state, and you should be, too."

Owen's face turned serious as he cleared his throat and answered, "Yes sir."

Exhilaration remained gleaming in the deputy's eyes, and it took all of Nick's patience not to throttle the man. He glanced at the cell phone resting in his hand. "It won't hurt them to wait for another minute or two. I have to make a phone call. I'll be out when I'm done."

"But sir..."

Nick shut the door on the deputy's wide eyes. He ran a hand down his face. *CNN?* He felt the throb of a new headache beginning at the base of his neck as he dialed Cali's number.

His anticipation grew with each passing ring. After the fifth one, her recorded voice came over the line. *"Leave me a message."*

He flipped the phone closed. It was probably too late anyway. He let out a long, slow breath. *Lord, I need your help now more than ever.*

Bracing himself for the onslaught of questions and flashing cameras, he grabbed his notes and headed outside into the blinding sun and warm afternoon temperatures. The reporters had set up their microphones in the middle of the parking lot. Surprised they had left enough room for anyone to park and maneuver around the crowd, Nick wondered if it was Deputy Owen's bright idea to set them up there, but kept the thought to himself.

He caught sight of Helen, standing off to the side. He motioned her toward him. "Take pictures of the crowd. The man we're looking for may decide to show up, looking like a concerned citizen."

"Gotcha." Helen disappeared inside the office to grab the camera.

He scanned the crowd, searching for anyone who looked as though they didn't belong. Numerous men and women stood around, most wearing some variety of press identification. A few curious tourists lingered in the back of the crowd, but none looked overly suspicious.

A surge of adrenaline swept through Nick when he spotted Cali across the parking lot, leaning against the hood of her silver-blue car. It may not be too late after all. Nick had not expected her to be there. He assumed she planned to watch the press conference on TV from her motel room. He should have known better.

Cali's hair was pulled back; a few loose tendrils framed her face. She held her arms crossed over the blue sundress she wore, and her eyes were hidden behind her fashionable sunglasses. She looked uncomfortable as she crossed her ankles first one way, then the next. Or maybe she was nervous. He couldn't blame her. He was nervous too.

Nick knew the moment Cali looked at him. He couldn't see her eyes through the dark lenses, but her lips curved into a hesitant smile. He wanted to smile back, to give her reassurance, but the reporters had run out of patience.

"How many women are missing? Do you have any suspects yet? Are you equipped to handle situations like this?" The questions bombarded him, some blending into the others. Forced to turn his focus away from Cali, he held his hands out to quiet the press.

"Thank you all for coming." He waited until they settled down before continuing, "I've called this press conference to enlist your help in the search for Serena Taylor. She is a twenty-seven-year-old woman who was reported missing from Coral Isle by a close friend on Sunday of this week, a day after she was supposed to have arrived back in her hometown of Brookstone, North Carolina. Ms. Taylor...Serena...is known to be responsible, and it is highly unlikely she went somewhere on her own without notifying her family or friends."

As Nick spoke, his nerves abated and he fell into his usual, authoritative and professional tone. "She's Caucasian, has dark-brown hair, and is five-foot-six-inches tall, weighing approximately one hundred-forty pounds. Witnesses have reported seeing her leave her oceanfront rental cottage alone late Friday evening wearing a yellow tank top and black Capri pants. She is thought to have been heading out to the beach for an evening walk."

As he spoke, he continually scanned the crowd. Helen stood off to the side, snapping photos from various angles. He was not surprised to see Deputy Owen standing to his left and a few steps behind him, directly in view of the CNN camera. Deputy Castle paced in the distance, keeping far away from the spotlight.

Nick's gaze returned to Cali. He had given

Serena's description and the basic details. Now it was time to make it personal. He wished he had time to ask Cali if it was OK with her. To prepare her. But, considering the reporters began murmuring and asking questions again, he knew his time had run out.

"Before I give further details, I'd like to ask Serena's close friend, Cali Stevens, to come forward and speak to you about who Serena is, and implore your assistance in finding her." He stepped to the side and held his hand out for Cali. Shock streaked across her face. But, with little hesitation, she straightened from her position on her car and walked toward Nick. Everyone turned to face her, but she kept her focus on him.

As she neared, Nick stepped forward, pressed his hand to her lower back, and leaned close. "I'm sorry for putting you on the spot. I wanted to ask you first but..."

"It's OK." Cali removed her sunglasses and met his eyes. "Thank you Sheriff. This means a lot to me." She spoke so low against the murmuring crowd that he barely made out the sincere words.

Stepping into the middle of the chaos, Cali turned to face the crowd. Nick wanted to follow her. He wanted to keep his hand on her lower back to reassure her, but from the way she stood straight and addressed the press, he knew she could stand on her own. He stood back, watching as his admiration grew.

"Good afternoon. My name is Cali Stevens, and I'm a close friend of Serena. I've known her for many years. I could tell you many things about her. I could tell you what you want to hear to make you sympathize with her. I could tell you she's a loving wife and mother. But she isn't. I could tell you she has a large family, with dozens of people waiting for her safe return. But she doesn't." Cali paused and took a deep breath. "The truth is she's single. She was an only child, and her parents both passed away by the time she was sixteen. My family took her in. Serena's like a sister to me. She's had a hard life, and in spite of everything she's been through, she's the first person to help someone in need. She's the most unselfish, caring person I know. She's also strong. She's a survivor. Serena, if you can hear me, don't give up. Fight back and fight hard. And for the coward who took her..."

Nick took her arm and firmly pulled her aside. "Thank you Ms. Stevens. Ms. H., will you see she returns safely to her car?"

Helen nodded. Judging by the scowl on Cali's face, she didn't care for being dismissed so easily. But, when Helen reached her side, Cali's features softened, and she turned and walked away without a fight.

Nick kept his gaze trained on Cali and Helen, waiting until they had walked a good distance away before saying, "Serena is the third woman on Coral Isle to be abducted by a serial rapist."

Cali stopped and swung around so fast she stumbled. Helen took her arm and steadied her, keeping her from falling. Nick assumed this was the first time she had heard the victims had been sexually assaulted. She slowly slid on her sunglasses, covering the tears welling in her eyes.

"Sheriff?" Deputy Owen brought his focus back to the hungry reporters.

He cleared his throat and drew his gaze from Cali. "We have reason to believe the abductor used GHB, commonly known as the date rape drug, to incapacitate his victims. GHB is odorless, colorless and besides a slightly salty taste, is virtually undetectable. Perpetrators often mix the drug with soda or alcoholic beverages, making it extremely difficult for the victim to discover the drug before it's too late.

"I want to assure the residents and visitors on

Coral Isle we're doing everything possible to find Serena, and to bring the criminal who abducted her to justice. And until we do, I'm asking every woman to be extremely cautious. Under no circumstances should you accept an open drink from anyone. It is also imperative you do not go anywhere alone. Close and lock your doors and windows, and stay alert to your surroundings at all times."

One of the reporters interrupted. "Sheriff Justice, what are you specifically doing to find the abductor?"

He acknowledged the reporter with a nod. "Although I cannot release any specific details of the investigation, I can tell you we have sent information developed from our investigation to the FBI. They will provide us with a criminal profile and check out any other offenses that appear to be related. I can also tell you we have obtained DNA samples of the offender from each of the first two victims. The DNA is being checked against the national database of convicted felons."

Voices erupted all around. Reporters clamored to get their questions answered above all the others. The resulting chaos made it impossible for Nick to answer even one more of the questions. Not that he had any more answers to give them anyway.

"That's all we have to tell you for now. We'll be posting any new information we can release on our website. A picture of Serena is already posted on the web. Please take a moment and look at it. If anyone has seen her or has any information regarding this case, contact our office."

He stepped away from the microphones before the reporters had a chance to swarm around him. He automatically looked for Cali, wanting to make sure she was all right. But, she had already climbed into her car. He glimpsed her pale face as she drove away, and recognized the devastation written across her features.

As a tide of remorse washed over him, he wondered if he should have warned her of the possibility of what may be happening to Serena. It may have softened the blow if he had told her last night over the phone. Then again, maybe it wouldn't have.

With renewed determination, he turned and stepped into his building, intent on tracking and putting away the predator who had dared pick Coral Isle as his hunting ground.

Chapter Ten

Serena is the third woman on Coral Isle to be abducted by a serial rapist. Close and lock your doors and windows. Don't go anywhere alone. Cali shivered as she remembered the words of warning Sheriff Justice gave to the women on Coral Isle.

Fear and anxiety built inside her, and the small, musty motel room didn't help. Her pulse raced. Her breathing became labored. She had to get out before claustrophobia descended, which would cause a full-blown panic attack.

She grabbed her room key and stepped outside. The warm, humid air did nothing to help her catch her breath, but the openness of being outside held the panic at bay.

"Ms. Stevens."

Cali jumped and twisted in one swift motion.

A man lounging on the bench seat in front of her room rose and stepped toward her. Her heartbeat intensified, and she took a hesitant step back. "Yes?"

He stopped. "Pardon my intrusion, ma'am. I didn't mean to startle you," the man said in a cautious tone. "My name's Lex Harrison. I'm a reporter for the Coral Isle Observer."

Cali steadied her breathing, and studied the press identification the middle-aged man held out. A strand of his long, thinning brown hair fell across his eyes, and he tucked it behind his ear. His teeth, too large for his mouth, shined as he smiled, and his bulbous nose crinkled as he studied her beneath dark lenses.

"You followed me."

His teeth disappeared into his mouth, but his lips remained curled. "Just looking for the truth. As a fellow reporter, I'm sure you understand."

"I don't have any information for you." She turned, heading for the beach.

Lex Harrison followed. "I have a proposition for you." He fell into step beside her.

"What are you talking about?"

"The sheriff seems to be a likeable guy, right?"

She stiffened and stopped walking. "What are you suggesting?"

"An alliance. You and me. You get the inside scoop on the investigation, and I get our names in the headlines."

"Let me get this straight. You want me to use the sheriff to get inside information so you'll get the publicity for it."

"Sure."

"Why would I want to do that?"

"I told you. Headlines. It would benefit both of us. Give our careers a boost."

"I don't need a career boost, and I'm not interested in headlines, unless they are the kind that says my friend has been found."

"I'm an opportunist, Ms. Stevens. I thought, as a reporter, you would be too. Isn't that why you are becoming friends with the sheriff?"

"You..." Several adjectives to describe the man came to her mind, but she refrained. "I'm not interested."

"Take my number." He held out a plain, black and white business card as his calculating gaze studied her. "In case you change your mind."

"The answer won't change." Cali took the thin,

inexpensive card and stuffed it into her back pocket, hoping he would back off and leave her alone.

"Good day to you, Ms. Stevens."

Relieved he had decided to leave, she said, "Goodbye, Mr. Harrison."

"Oh, and be careful out there. You never know who you might run into."

Unease crept up her spine at the unexpected warning. "I'm always cautious."

His bushy brows lifted. "Really? Yet, you didn't see me coming did you?"

He turned and walked away, leaving her with the sting of his words. He had followed her, probably straight from the press conference, and she hadn't even noticed.

Anxious to put the incident out of her mind, Cali headed across the road to the beach, hoping to find solace in the calming sounds of the ocean. After walking for a few minutes, her breathing returned to normal as the sounds of the waves crashing against the shoreline soothed her, helping her escape from reality for a few precious moments. As the evening progressed, she kept her mind focused on the simple act of putting one sandy foot in front of the other and let all other thoughts be carried away.

The sun sank low on the horizon, casting a soft, amber glow to the surface of Coral Isle. She passed by a young couple, strolling hand-in-hand along the foamy surf, oblivious to the chaos consuming Cali's life. She continued past them, looking to the beach that lay beyond. A large brown sign came into view, clearly marking the beginning of the Coral Isle Nature Preserve. No one occupied the beach beyond the notice, and she relished the idea of a few moments alone.

Cali fell into a rhythm, walking along the shoreline as the waves continued to grow deeper, stretching along the beach farther and farther up as the tide worked its way in. The beach became thinner, the passageway between the ocean and dunes narrower. Afraid of being squeezed out of walking space, she stopped for a moment to breathe in the salty sea air and embrace the solitude before heading back.

When she turned, she immediately recognized she had gone farther than she had planned. She glanced at her watch and discovered she had been walking close to an hour and a half. How far had she gone along on the deserted beach? Alarmed by the discovery she had traveled too far, the sun seemed to hasten its decent, taking its calming amber glow with it and casting long shadows on the sand that lay ahead. The grayness of twilight descended, and she felt a prickly unease crawl along her spine. Every hair on her neck stood on end. Cali had the distinct feeling someone was watching her.

She wanted to brush off her apprehension, to attribute it to the darkening sky, yet she'd learned to trust her instincts years ago. Using them now, she picked up speed, launching into a full jog.

She cast several quick glances over her shoulder. No one was behind her, and no one in front. There was no evidence to support her sudden unease. But, when she had covered about a quarter of a mile, she sensed a presence some distance behind her. A dark presence, and it felt wrong. Extremely wrong.

As the sky darkened, panic consumed her.

Cali ran as fast and hard as she could, yet felt as if she moved in slow motion as the sand slowed her progress. Her breathing quickly became labored, her lungs screamed for oxygen. She used her initial surge of adrenaline in record time, yet was awarded with a second surge when she peeked over her shoulder again and a bright light blinded her.

"Cali?"

She heard her name spoken in a question, yet it sounded foreign. She couldn't see past the light to identify the source of the voice. *He knows my name! The stalker knows my name!* The second round of adrenaline shot through her system and she took off faster, nearly tripping over the depressions and grooves in the sand.

She prayed for help. She prayed for protection.

"Wait!"

Urgency resounded in the deep voice. A man's deep voice. Terror filled her, taking control of all rational thoughts. *Move faster. Move faster.* The frightening thoughts kept her legs moving, when her sides started to ache and her deep breaths turned into uncontrolled fits of coughing.

Heavy footsteps came close behind her, and she struggled to outdistance them. Precious seconds later, a strong arm banded around her waist, lifting her off the ground and back against a hard, solid chest. Cali screamed for help, but feared she had ventured too far out for anyone to hear. She struggled, panting for breath. She kicked, scratched and turned her head to bite a well-muscled shoulder.

"Cali," he spoke her name in an even, controlled tone.

A spark of recognition hit her, but before she had time to place exactly who it was, the man dropped the flashlight into the sand and twisted her around.

"It's me. Sheriff Justice. It's OK. You're OK." He held her by her shoulders, steadying her as she fought to gain her balance.

"Sheriff?" She recognized the outline of his features, and the hard angle of his jaw. "Justice." All at once, the feeling of something being terribly wrong vanished. It was quickly replaced with a sense of calmness and security. Cali wrapped her arms around his waist and leaned into the firm length of his body. She buried her head under his chin, feeling his strong heartbeat against her cheek as she rested against his chest. She noticed he had replaced his standard uniform with a pair of jeans and a dark, snug-fitting T-shirt, and he smelled fresh out of the shower, as if soap still clung to his skin. His masculine scent surrounded her, providing a more intimate layer of comfort.

He enfolded her into his arms, but the tension remained in his body. "I saw you running. Something scared you."

"*Someone* scared me."

He pulled back, placing his hands on her shoulders. "Did you see somebody?"

She looked into his intense eyes. "N-no." She shook her head. "But I felt someone nearby, and it wasn't you."

"Are you sure?" He glanced over his shoulder, then his gaze came back to drill into hers.

"I'm sure. I felt something..." she hesitated, afraid of what he may think of her relying purely on instinct.

"Something what?" he prodded.

"Out of place. Something just plain wrong." She shivered as goose bumps traveled up her arms and neck. She looked away into the churning sea, not wanting to see doubt in his eyes.

He ran his warm, solid hands down her arms, and then lifted his hand to cup her face. Using his thumb, he coaxed her chin up until she had no recourse but to meet his questioning gaze. When she discovered no doubt, no ridicule, relief swept over her, urging her to say, "And I don't feel that when I'm with you. I feel safe with you."

Something flashed across the deep-blue depths of his eyes. His gaze flickered to her lips and he hesitated, before dropping his hand and leaning to recover the flashlight.

He took her arm in his urgent grasp and began walking with her. "I'll take you to my truck. It's on the road directly past this dune. When we get there, get inside and lock the doors. I'm going to look for him."

"Do you think it's the stalker?" she asked, breathless from running and then trying to keep up with his long strides.

"There's a good chance it is."

They climbed the path up the sand dune and he loosened his grip, sliding his hand to lace his fingers with hers. Stepping in front on the narrow passageway, he half dragged her up the slope in his haste. When they crested the hill, Cali was surprised to find the road right next to the dune. She spotted the white truck, marked "Sheriff of Coral Isle."

Nick led her to the truck, using the remote to unlock it. Opening the door, he guided her into the passenger seat with his hands on her waist and slammed the door. The locks engaged before she had a chance to find the inside control panel and lock them first. He stopped long enough to nod his head, his eyes telling her to stay put. She nodded back, watching his determination surge forth. He turned, drew his pistol from his ankle holster and disappeared into the dark night in search of a stalker.

Chapter Eleven

Nick welcomed the adrenaline rushing through his system. It gave him additional energy as he combed the grassy dunes looking for the source of Cali's fear. He had no doubt her instincts had been right. Someone had been out here, but his hopes of finding the person diminished with every passing moment.

He searched the shoreline, shining his light into the darkness. The beam highlighted the sand and swirling ocean water, but he found no one lurking in the shadows. He didn't want to leave Cali for too long, or go too far away from her, so he turned and headed back over the dunes. When he approached the side of the road, he looked for tire tracks in the sand that had not been swept away by the constant ocean breeze. He found none.

By the time Nick returned to his truck, his fear for Cali's safety had switched into a low, simmering anger. He climbed in, slammed the door shut and locked them inside the cab. "What were you doing out here alone?"

"Taking a walk."

He clenched his jaw and blood pounded through his veins. "Taking a walk? Didn't anything I said during the press conference sink in?"

"Of course it did. That's why I came out here to

begin with."

He scoffed, "I think you'd better explain that one to me real quick. I have a mind to throw you into a cell and lock you up until this whole thing is over."

"I came out to the beach to sort things out. You...you released some details I wasn't expecting to hear." Cali gripped the handle on the passenger door and inched away.

Nick noticed her defensive gesture but chose to ignore it. "I left plenty of details out. You have no idea what this man could do to you. And you nearly walked right into his hands."

Her eyes widened. "Did you see him? Was he out here?"

"I didn't see him. But he was here."

"If you didn't see him, how do you know?"

"The same way you did. Gut instinct." He held his temper in check, but considering the danger Cali had exposed herself to, he had a hard time keeping his voice steady. "When I first met you, I thought you had a good head on your shoulders. I guess I was wrong." Nick shoved the key into the ignition and revved the engine. He let it idle for a moment. "Do you *want* to be his next target?"

"No. Of course not." Cali crossed her arms over her chest. "I didn't realize how far I'd walked on the beach. Then it started getting dark..."

"Providing the perfect opportunity for him to grab you," he snapped as a new anger burned inside. "Do me a favor. The next time you're looking for the big story to jump-start your career, do it somewhere else."

Her clear-blue eyes clouded over, making her look like a wounded doe. She shrank away, and a glimmer of moisture welled in her eyes. "I would never..." her voice cracked.

Nick instantly regretted his words. He had seen her desperate flight on the beach. He didn't believe she would intentionally put herself in danger for a story, but he had seen such foolish acts before.

He gritted his teeth as he put the truck in drive and pulled out onto the deserted highway. He concentrated on the road ahead, trying to give time for the magnetic force of the woman sitting next to him to lessen. After a few minutes, he realized it wasn't working. If anything, the pull became stronger. Nick glanced her way. She had her head turned, looking out the side window with the wounded look showing through her profile. Though she kept her back straight, she'd let her arms drop to her lap, and clasped her hands in front of her. One of the thin straps on her sundress had slipped unheeded down her shoulder, and he had a sudden urge to slip it back into place. He gripped the steering wheel tighter, so he would not give in to the temptation to touch her.

His gaze flickered from the road back to her face. With her defenses down, a hint of innocence showed through, and a touch of vulnerability became exposed. Nick felt his heart slide a notch.

"Look, I didn't mean..." He sighed in frustration, unsure of how to make things right between them, and wondering why he wanted so badly to see her smile. "I'm only trying to protect you."

Cali didn't respond, merely stared out into the darkness.

The silence in the truck only served to heighten Nick's tension, causing a low throbbing ache to begin at the base of his neck. He rolled his shoulders to ease his tight muscles and glanced her way once more. She remained pressed against the side door, much like she had pressed against him on the beach. The memory of how soft and feminine she had felt stirred emotions he had kept hidden for a long time. Emotions he could not afford to let surface now, not with a stalker on the loose and an entire island of people to protect.

As Nick pulled into the driveway at the Sea

Urchin, his protective instincts overpowered his common sense. "I don't like that you're staying here alone. I have a cottage near the northern tip of the island. I live on the bottom floor and rent the top half to families on vacation. Right now, I don't have any renters. You could come and stay there."

Her mouth dropped open, then shut again. Indecision played across her features. Instead of answering his offer she asked, "If you live on the northern tip of the island, what were you doing at the nature preserve? It's as far south as you can get."

Nick claimed a parking spot directly in front of her motel room. He put the truck in park and switched off the ignition. Studying her, he discovered no underlying suspicion in her gaze, heard none in her voice. She trusted him. So, he would give her a little bit of trust back. "I was searching for the kidnapper. I didn't mention this in the press conference, but the women who were abducted each turned up on the dunes at the southern shores. He released both of them at night, at high tide."

"High tide? Why?"

He shrugged. "He called using a pre-paid cell phone. Both times. Told us where to find the victims. It's almost as if he's afraid something will happen to them after he releases them." He hadn't meant to give her details, or add his opinion to the mix, but the more time he spent with her, the more he wanted to share. Abruptly ending the discussion, he stepped out and walked around to open the door.

When Cali hesitated, he gently took her hand and urged her to climb from the truck. Her face paled as she asked, "Did he call about Serena? Is that why you were out there?"

"No." Surprised by the regret he heard in his own voice he continued, "I'm sorry. I went out there hoping to catch him in case he changed his routine and released her early."

A tinge of color returned to Cali's cheeks as he walked her to the door. "How many nights have you been out there searching?" She pulled the room key from her pocket and looked at him.

"Every night since Ms. Taylor…Serena has been missing."

Cali took in a sharp breath. "Then I owe you an apology," she admitted.

"For what?"

"For accusing you of not caring about her and the rest of the people on this island. You do care don't you?"

"Yes. I do."

Softness entered her gaze before she looked away. She tried to slip the key into the door, but the shaking in her hands prevented her from matching the key to the keyhole.

Nick rested a hand over hers, squeezing gently. "Let me help."

She placed the key in his palm, but he didn't attempt to open the door. Instead, he stepped closer, cupped her face in his hand and gently stroked her cheek with his thumb. Her skin felt smooth and soft beneath his calloused touch. He lifted her face until their eyes met. "Come with me. Let me protect you." His voice came out raspy and low.

"I-It's late. I should stay here and go to bed."

A blush rose up her neck and expanded to cover both cheeks. The innocent reaction caused an electrifying jolt through his system, filling him with a strong desire to feel her pressed against him again. He lowered his gaze to her lips, wanting to comfort her and ease the tremble in them. Wanting to taste them. When her lips parted slightly, he bent his head lower, the temptation to kiss her growing in intensity. He felt her warm breath on his skin, and smelled her sweet scent. Roses. She smelled like roses. Why had he not noticed before?

A door slamming nearby brought reality crashing back. Cali had been through a scare tonight. A scare that had left her shaken and confused. He had no business taking advantage of her. At the last second before his lips touched hers, he lifted them to her forehead instead, and pressed them against her soft skin. He dropped his hand to his side as he took a step back.

"You've been through a lot in the past few days. You should try to get some sleep."

Cali ran a hand through her wind-tossed hair, and he stifled the urge to run his own hand through her thick, wavy strands. When she looked at the door, he remembered he still held the key, and unlocked the door with a surprisingly steady hand. Nick flipped on the light, and acting on instinct, searched the room to make sure no one was there.

Without a word, he checked the bathroom, discovering it was safe, but in worse shape than he expected. He had been called to the Sea Urchin to settle a few domestic disputes in the past, but each time he had been able to resolve problems from the outside, and had not had the pleasure of experiencing the reason for the motel's poor reputation.

Nick had not expected to see the broken tiles on the walls and the peeling linoleum on the floor. The only things in the room that did not look outdated were Cali's personal items. A pink razor sat on the edge of the tub, and the bottle of shower gel sitting next to it had a bouquet of roses decorating the front label, no doubt the source of her alluring scent. As Nick turned to leave the room, he glanced at the small sink. Cali's make-up bag rested on the cracked porcelain. It had a small pink heart embroidered on the side, feminine and delicate, reminding him of its owner.

Nick turned and stepped into the main room, sweeping his gaze across the remainder of the interior. The dark stains on the shabby carpet appeared to be several years old, and the cheap, framed pictures on the walls were yellowed and warped. The old, scarred furniture pieces were mixed in color, as if they had been bought piecemeal at a thrift store.

Nick tucked his thumbs into the pockets of his jeans. "You deserve a better place to stay than this." He continued to look around the room. Cali's suitcase rested on the bed nearest the door, with its contents neatly arranged inside. A laptop sat next to it, along with a well-used notepad. He sensed Cali watching him and resisted the urge to read the words scribbled across the pages. Instead, he looked at her and asked, "Will you reconsider and come home with me?"

She appeared to think about his offer, but after a moment shook her head. "The room's already paid for. I should stay here tonight."

"Are you always this stubborn?"

A slight smile touched her lips. "Usually."

Sighing, Nick stepped close, catching the sweet scent radiating around her. This time, he did not resist the urge to slip the forgotten strap on her sundress back on her shoulder. His fingers brushed her warm, soft skin. He could have imagined it, but he thought he felt her lean into his brief touch.

"I do appreciate the offer, Sheriff." Cali sounded breathless. Her chest rose and fell in a quick, nervous rhythm.

"No problem. And Cali...there's no need for formalities between us. Call me Nick."

"OK. Nick."

He liked the way his name sounded coming from her lips. Maybe a little bit too much. He cleared his throat and took a step back to make sure he wouldn't touch her again. Withdrawing a business card from his back pocket, he handed it to her. He should tell her to call the station if anything happened. To call if she remembers anything that could help the investigation. He should tell her again to leave and go home. But, the only words he wanted to say were more personal.

"My home and cell numbers are written on the back. Call me anytime, day or night." Nick stepped around her and through the open door, turning back he added, "Lock up tight. Goodnight."

Nick headed for his truck, wondering if he should even leave her the choice of staying at the motel. Driving out of the parking lot, he considered turning around, packing her bags, stuffing her into the passenger seat, and not letting her out of his sight again until the stalker was tucked away behind steel bars.

Chapter Twelve

Cali woke to warm sunlight filtering through the thin, dusty curtains. She peeled her eyes open to check the time, but something shiny on the lamp above the clock caught her attention.

She recognized Serena's silver necklace draped across the old, faded lampshade. Terror immobilized her, preventing her from moving a muscle. She tried to scream, but no sound erupted from her throat.

Nick.

Adrenaline shot into her veins, providing the strength to take action. She searched her purse and found the card with his number. She grabbed her phone and dialed his cell, but her hands trembled so violently she had to press end and re-dial the number.

"Sheriff Justice," he answered on the second ring.

"N-Nick. He's been here. Inside my room." Her words shook as heavily as her hands.

After only a moment's hesitation he answered, "Get out. Now. I'm on my way." Rustling came across the line as if he were already in motion.

Her breath caught. Her gaze darted across the room. *Lord, the intruder might still be inside! Keep me safe!* She tugged the sheet from the bed, wrapping it around her nightgown as she stood. Her cell phone landed on the carpet with a dull thud. Cali ignored it as she scrambled for the door. She yanked it open and fled outside with her heart pounding and blood rushing through her ears.

Outside, everything appeared normal, contrasting the chaos running through her mind. Cali searched for anyone or anything unusual. She appeared to be the only one out of place, standing on the walkway wrapped in a thin, white sheet. Another motel guest came out of a room a few doors down and gave her a curious glance before turning and walking in the opposite direction.

Cali started to head for the pool area to wait for Nick, but the sounds of children laughing and splashing inside the pool kept her from venturing toward it. In case the stalker had not left yet, she didn't want to put anyone else in danger, especially not children, so she settled onto a bench seat and waited.

Her cell phone rang. Not daring to retrieve it, she let it continue to ring.

"Did you see anyone suspicious?"

Cali jumped and turned. Deputy Owen stood behind her, breathing heavily with his hand resting on top of his pistol.

"I didn't see you drive up. Where did you come from?"

"I was across the street at Miller's Restaurant having breakfast." He gestured behind the motel. "The sheriff called, told me what happened. Did you see anyone?" he repeated the question as he crept to the opened door.

"No."

"Stay here." He drew his pistol and disappeared into the room.

Her heart beat as if she were running a marathon. She stood, preparing to flee if the stalker came barreling outside.

A moment later, Deputy Owen strolled out. "It's

clear." He holstered his pistol, hitched up his belt and placed his hands on his hips.

Cali released a sigh and let the tension ease from her muscles.

"Are you OK?"

"I'm not hurt." She wouldn't be honest if she answered "yes." She was too shaken to be OK.

Her cell phone rang again. She headed toward the room, but nearly ran into Deputy Owen's outstretched arm as he blocked the doorway.

"Be careful not to touch anything but your phone."

"OK."

He dropped his arm, stepped to the side, and let her pass. Cali scooped her cell phone from the floor and sat on the edge of the bed to answer it, but the phone stopped ringing. The necklace caught her attention before she had a chance to check who had called. Tears gathered in her eyes and rolled down her cheeks. *Lord, where is Serena? What has he done to her?*

The bed shifted as Deputy Owen sat next to her. He wrapped an arm around her shoulders. His sleek gaze slid across the white sheet she wore, making her shiver.

"It's all right. I'm here. You're safe now."

Obviously, he had misread the reason she trembled. The soft words sounded hollow and self-righteous coming from the arrogant man. She tried to pull away, not the least bit comforted by his presence, but he did not release her.

"I sure am glad I was close by. If you'd had to wait for the sheriff..." He glanced at his watch and shook his head.

Cali narrowed her gaze as irritation spiked her blood pressure, and spurred a sudden, driving need to defend Nick. "I'm sure he'll get here as fast as he can."

She was about to insist Deputy Owen let her go

when tires squealed and then a vehicle door slammed. A moment later Nick ran in, gun drawn and ready.

Deputy Owen spoke up, "It's all clear sir." His arm remained around Cali.

Nick noticed.

The concern on his features switched to irritation as his gaze flicked from Deputy Owen to Cali. He tucked his gun into an ankle holster under his jeans, crossed his arms and waited.

Cali pulled away from the deputy. This time he let her go. She wanted to launch into Nick's arms. She wanted to feel safe again. But, judging from the hard look on his face, she assumed he was in no mood to comfort her.

"Tell me what happened."

She stood, dried her wet cheeks, and squared her shoulders. "The stalker broke in sometime during the night. I didn't hear anything. I didn't even know until this morning." She turned and pointed to the lampshade. "He left Serena's necklace hanging here."

Deputy Owen stood and walked toward the door. "I have to go get my cruiser. I left it in the restaurant's lot. I'll be right back."

Nick ignored Owen and walked over to peer at the necklace. "Are you sure it's hers?"

Cali stepped behind him. "I'm positive."

"Is anything missing?"

The question took her off guard. "I don't know. I haven't checked. Deputy Owen said not to touch anything."

Nick walked past her and scanned the bathroom. When he came back he said, "Go ahead and check your belongings. Make sure nothing is missing or has been disturbed."

His tone of voice sounded official, and she checked her duffle bag and suitcase without question. "It looks like it's all here." She looked up to find Nick inspecting the doorframe.

"He didn't use force."

"Then how did he get inside?"

"He either picked the locks," Nick knelt in front of the doorknob and continued, "or he had two keys."

"Two keys?"

"There's one key for the doorknob, and another for the deadbolt, which is probably a master key."

Cali shivered even though the day had already begun to warm, making the room stuffy and humid. The air-conditioner unit continued to rattle, unsuccessfully trying to cool the room with the door wide open. She sat on the bed and covered her face with her hands as her fears deepened. She prayed, *Lord, thank you for protecting me last night. Please continue to watch over us.*

"Cali." Nick's voice was close.

She felt his hand on her hair, sweeping to the nape of her neck. Then his hand slid to her shoulder as he sat next to her. She reacted to Nick's touch completely different than she had to Deputy Owen. This time, she leaned into the embrace. This time she felt safe.

"Why would he break in here to leave the necklace and not take me, too?" Cali asked as she lifted her head, finding Nick's features full of concern. "It doesn't make any sense."

He pulled his arm away and stood, shaking his head. "It's hard to tell. It could be a way to threaten you. A warning for you to stay away from the investigation. Or, it could be his way of showing off. He's gaining confidence with each woman he takes without being caught. No matter what the reason is, I'm glad you're safe."

Deputy Owen strode back into the room without warning. Nick addressed the deputy, his no-nonsense demeanor returning immediately. "I'll take Cali outside while you take photographs of the room. Be careful when you collect the necklace. Make sure the lab checks for more than fingerprints. I want any and all possible evidence identified from it. I want to know if it's really hers."

Deputy Owen clenched his jaw as if he resented following Nick's orders. But, he turned and went outside without a word.

"I told you it's Serena's necklace."

Nick swung around. "I know you think it is, but I need verifiable proof."

A pang of irritation hit her and she lifted her chin. "My word isn't proof enough?"

He sighed, running a hand through his hair. "Serena was wearing the necklace in the picture released to the press. Anyone who saw it could have found a necklace resembling hers and decide to play a prank on you."

She sucked in a breath. "Do you think that's what happened?"

"No. I don't. But I have to be sure. Come on. Let's go outside and wait."

"Can't I get dressed first?"

"After the photos are taken." Nick took her arm and led her out the door.

Curious guests had gathered around the area. Owen was talking to a young woman clad in a skimpy bikini when Nick called to him. "Deputy."

Owen swung around and said, "Right. I'm on it."

"There's nothing interesting going on here folks. Move on." Nick motioned for the small crowd to disperse. Most of them did, but one man walking toward them kept on coming.

Cali recognized the white-haired owner of the motel from five rooms away. He shuffled along the walkway with a clear purpose in mind. She wondered exactly what that purpose was until he walked right to Nick and said, "I don't need no trouble here. What's going on?"

Nick flashed his badge and addressed the aging man. "Are you the owner?"

"Yes sir, I am. Name's Stoley. Tom Stoley."

The men shook hands.

"Someone broke in to Ms. Stevens's room last night."

Tom Stoley's eyes widened. "We haven't had a break in for several years now." His brow furrowed as he cast a suspicious glance at Cali. "What for?"

Cali's defenses rose. "It wasn't my fault."

Nick stepped between them. "I have some questions for you, Mr. Stoley. Then we'll be on our way."

Nick led Mr. Stoley down a corridor housing the vending and ice machines. Cali couldn't hear their words as they rounded the corner.

Obviously, Nick intended to cut her out of the conversation. Irritation spiked deep inside. "Oh, no you don't." She turned and ran to catch up. The cement walkway scuffed her bare feet and the sand felt like grit under her skin, but she ignored the minor annoyance.

As she approached, both men looked up as if she were the intruder. She had to speak unusually loud to combat the hum radiating from the ice machine. "A man came into my room last night Mr. Stoley." She would have plopped her hands on her hips if she weren't still holding the sheet around her body. "Exactly how secure do you keep your room keys?"

Nick shot her a steely glare before saying, "Excuse me for a moment sir. I'll be right back." His gaze stayed locked onto Cali as he swept toward her. Each of the three steps he had to take was rigid and filled with determination.

Nick came within inches, glaring. "Go back." A muscle twitched in his jaw and his eyes blazed.

"I have a right to know."

"You'll have a right to remain silent if you don't move. Now."

Judging from the scowl on his face, she did not doubt him for a second. Cali gave the owner one last

glance before walking back to the bench.
****

Nick tried hard not to lose his temper. After Cali had put Mr. Stoley on the defensive, the motel owner became unreasonably tight-lipped. Other than insisting no one could have possibly gotten their hands on his room keys, the man turned out to be no help at all.

Nick clenched his teeth as he rounded the corner to face Cali. She was gone. "Owen. Where is she?"

The deputy slammed the trunk on his cruiser and came around to the front. "She's changing clothes."

"Take the evidence in. I want answers."

"Will do."

Nick paced in front of Cali's motel door as Owen drove away. He took a few deep breaths, trying to calm his frustration. It didn't work. He still had his fists clenched when the door opened behind him.

"Do you have any idea what you just did?" He turned, prepared to set Cali straight.

"I want answers as much as you do, Sheriff." The cool, controlled tone of voice she used did not fool him. Her eyes betrayed her. She was still shaken from the incident.

Nick fought against the compassion tugging at him and kept his voice stern. "Yes. I know you do. But, there are right ways to go about getting those answers. Offending someone isn't one of them."

"I think someone could've gotten a copy of Mr. Stoley's keys, and he doesn't want to admit it."

"Maybe. But we won't know for sure now that you've put him on the defense."

She tilted her head. "What's the matter? Can't you finesse it out of him like everyone else you meet?"

"Where'd you get that idea?"

"Helen. She said you can talk through tough situations with finesse. What's different about this one?"

He stepped closer, his carefully controlled temper flared. "I'll tell you what's different. You. By stepping into the middle of my investigation, you've put yourself right where you don't belong. And today, you've caused more harm than good."

Cali looked away for a moment, crossing her arms. Then, she returned her gaze to his. "I didn't mean to cause any harm. I just wanted..."

"Wanted what?"

"An answer that would take away the fear I've felt since waking up this morning."

Nick's heart jolted. His anger dissipated. The compassion he had tried to hold at bay returned with a vengeance.

"If I knew the stalker got a hold of the motel keys, I'd feel much safer than if he had the skill to pick the locks. If he can pick locks, I'm not safe anywhere."

"I'll keep you safe," the words slipped out before he had a chance to think it through. *Dear God, please help me be able to keep my promise.*

Cali rubbed her hands up and down her arms. "How?"

"You're coming to my cottage. That's how."

Her eyes widened and she held up a hand. "You don't have to..."

"I know I don't have to."

She tilted her head. "Why would you take me in? Why not just try and make me go home to Brookstone?"

"Because I know you wouldn't go. Even if I took you there myself, you'd come back."

"You're right," she admitted.

"So, the best way to keep you safe is to keep you close to me."

"Look, I appreciate the gesture. But, I can..."

"You're coming with me, Cali." He took a step toward her.

"But..."

"Why resist? I'll use my finesse on you until you agree."

A faint smile sprang to her lips. "Very funny. But, I don't like being somewhere I'm not wanted."

"I do want you." Nick cleared his throat, shifted his weight from one foot to the other and added, "To stay at my cottage. It's the safest place for you." But, he wanted her to stay close for more reasons than to protect her. "Pack your bags. You can ride with me."

"What about my car?"

"I'll make sure it gets to my cottage."

"I can drive."

He touched her hand. "You're still shaking. Besides, I'm not going straight home. You can come with me, and I'll get you settled in later." He gave her fingers a gentle squeeze.

"I had plans today."

"Plans change. Get your stuff. I'm heading over to a friend's house to check on her."

"A friend?"

"Yeah. I believe you'll like her."

"She won't mind?" Cali asked hesitantly.

"It's not a date, if that's what you're worried about."

He detected a flicker of relief cross her features before she agreed.

It only took Cali a few minutes to pack, and Nick helped her load her items into the backseat of his truck. He helped her into the passenger side, and then climbed in.

"You scared me when I couldn't reach you on the phone. I called twice. Why didn't you pick up?" He cranked the ignition and set the air conditioner to high, in hopes of combating the rising temperatures.

"I dropped my cell phone in the room when you told me to get out. I heard it ringing but was afraid to go back in and get it. I'm sorry I scared you."

Nick blew out a breath and relaxed. He rolled

his left shoulder, trying to ease the persistent ache. "It's OK. You did right by not going back in there."

He remembered the sting of jealousy when he had arrived and found Owen's arm around Cali. He didn't have the right to be jealous, but he was. "When did Deputy Owen arrive?"

"Right after I called you. He said he was having breakfast at a place nearby, and that's how he got here so fast." She hesitated and hugged her arms. "Nick, do you trust him?"

He shrugged. "Yes. With the things that matter."

"Things that matter?"

"He can be presumptuous at times, and cocky. But when it comes to his job, he's good at it. Why do you ask?"

"Never mind."

"Tell me."

"I'm just uncomfortable being alone with him."

His protective instincts kicked in. "What did he do?"

"Nothing. Not really."

"Cali, if he was inappropriate with you, I need to know."

"He wasn't. I just didn't like being alone with him."

The relief he felt shouldn't have been so intense, but knowing Cali's feelings toward Deputy Owen made Nick realize his bout with jealousy was over nothing. He backed out of the parking spot and pulled out onto the beach road heading north.

"I hadn't planned on coming out this way today since I'm off duty. I was at home when you called. I got to you as soon as I could."

"I know you did. I'm not blaming you for anything. Deputy Owen just happened to be closer than you at the time."

He shook his head and tightened his grip on the wheel. "I should never have asked you to speak at the press conference. The stalker must have seen you. I put you in danger." The responsibility for his rash decision weighed heavily on his shoulders.

"You don't know that. The guy could have seen me somewhere else."

"It's possible. But I doubt it," he argued.

"Don't blame yourself, Nick. It won't do any good. What's done is done."

"I'm surprised to hear you say that when you shoulder so much blame yourself."

"I don't know what you're talking about." She looked away.

He pulled the truck to a stop on the side of the road, cupped her chin and gently brought her focus back. "I'm talking about how you regret not coming with Serena. Isn't that why you won't leave the island and trust me to do my job?"

"I..." She took a deep breath. "I don't know what I feel right now besides being scared from the break-in and scared for Serena. I hate not knowing what's happening."

"And, you blame yourself for her abduction."

Cali pushed his hand away yet kept her simmering gaze on him. "So what if I do?"

"Then I'd say you have major control issues, and you need to learn your limitations."

A blush rose up her cheeks, and she looked out the side window.

Guilt nudged him. "Cali, I didn't mean to be so blunt. Sometimes I say things before..."

"You've talked about limitations before," she interrupted. "You said you learned a long time ago you have them. What happened?"

Returning his gaze to the road, Nick contemplated the wisdom in revealing his past. He had wanted to tell her when they had disagreed on the beach to prove a point, but now second thoughts made him hesitate. He hadn't told anyone about the incident in a long time and was not sure if he was prepared to do it now.

The silence stretched as he maneuvered the truck back onto the road and through the interior of the island. Weaving through the back roads, he took the shortest route to the west side. When they arrived at their destination, a small, one story cottage on the bay, he pulled into the driveway and cut the engine.

Cali looked at him. "It's OK. You don't have to tell me what happened."

Nick glanced her way. "I haven't told anyone about it in a long time." He felt his resolve weakening when he met her eyes. "You really want to know?"

"Of course."

"All right. Then I'll show you." Nick stepped out of the truck and came around to open the passenger side door. He knew he was risking becoming vulnerable by exposing his past, but he lifted his hand and helped her out anyway, preparing himself for her reaction.

Chapter Thirteen

Breathe. Cali stood, mesmerized by Nick's bare chest, as she took in his tanned, muscular physique. She tried to adjust to the fact Nick had just stripped his navy blue T-shirt off right in front of her.

Then her gaze landed on the scar.

She reached for his left shoulder, to touch the jagged remains of what looked like it had been a gaping wound, but he shifted away.

"This," Nick pointed to the scar, "is what reminds me every day I have limitations, and I cannot control every situation that comes my way." He turned. The scar continued six inches down the back of his shoulder.

Cali took a hesitant step across the graveled drive. This time as she reached for him, he didn't pull away. His skin felt warm to her fingertips as she traced the scar from beginning to end. Goose bumps broke out on his arms and across his back in spite of the warm day. He stilled as she pressed her palm against the worst of the scarring, and his firm muscles tensed beneath her touch.

"What happened?" Her voice cracked.

He covered her hand with his. "A few years ago, we got a call for a dispute at the Haven Inn. It's a popular oceanfront hotel with a bar that stays open until 4:00 a.m. On occasion, we'll be called in when someone's gone over their drink limit and has gotten out of hand. That night, a group of college guys got into a fight over a girl. I was off duty at the time the call came in, but I was only two blocks away. So, I decided to go. Without backup. I thought I could handle it on my own. I was wrong."

He stepped away. Cali's hand fell to her side. She crossed her arms and prepared for what he might say next.

"I should've known better than to go in alone the moment I saw three guys in a fist fight."

"What did you do?"

He shrugged. "I stepped into the middle of it."

"And one of them had a knife?"

"Yep."

She sucked in a breath. "Oh, Nick."

"I had one guy cuffed and searched right away. I turned to break up the other two, but one of them pulled out a switchblade. He waved it around, threatening everyone close to him. The crowd scattered." Nick closed his eyes as if recalling the scene in detail. "It wasn't safe to pull my gun. I knew I couldn't get a clean shot." He shook his head and looked at her. "I should've waited for backup."

"But you couldn't have known one of them would have a knife. How many tourists walk around armed?"

"You'd be surprised." Nick ran a hand over his face, stepped to the side, and then leaned against his truck. "I was born and raised here. I started my law enforcement career here, but I wanted to experience the big city life for awhile. I'd just come back from working in the Las Vegas P.D. for four years when this happened. I thought I'd seen everything. I thought I could handle anything that could possibly happen on Coral Isle on my own."

"So you discovered your limitations."

"That's right. My pride took a hit, and I learned a little bit about humility." He shrugged and pulled on his shirt. "And I realized God created us to need each other. We weren't made to carry the load alone, Cali. We need help from God and each other."

"So the guy with the knife came after you?"

"No. He went after the girl he couldn't have."

Cali gasped. "Oh, no."

"I saw his intentions and pushed her out of the way."

"Then he stabbed you instead," she spoke her assumptions aloud.

Nick winced, as if recalling the initial pain.

"I don't understand how people can do such things." She shivered and glanced at his shoulder again. "Does it still hurt?"

"Every day."

Cali wanted to help heal the emotional wounds that must remain along with the physical, but didn't have a clue as to where to start or what to say. So, she said the first thing that came to mind. "That sucks."

It startled her when Nick threw his head back and laughed, revealing a brilliant smile. "That's a first. Most people come up with some sort of sappy condolence or a look of pity."

She couldn't help but smile back as her sullen mood instantly lifted. She shrugged and tilted her head. "What can I say? I tell it like it is. I guess it's a side effect of being a reporter."

"I guess so. But it's a refreshing side effect."

"That's a roundabout compliment."

"No. It's a direct compliment." His eyes sparkled as his smile widened.

She felt a subtle shift in the atmosphere, and it wasn't due to the weather. She sucked in a little extra air with her next breath, trying to remain poised under his unexpected flattery.

Nick slowly drew his gaze away and looked toward the small, beige cottage. "We'd better go in. Mrs. Mayes is probably peeking out the window by now, wondering what we're doing."

"Mrs. Mayes?"

"She's a widower. Her two sons live out of state, so I come by to check on her from time to time."

"How did you meet her?"

"She's a member of my church." They stepped side-by-side onto the weathered porch. Nick turned. "Don't be surprised if she thinks we're together. She's been after me for years to get hitched."

Her face warmed at the thought of her and Nick as a couple. She fought to keep her voice calm. "A matchmaker, huh?"

"Very much so. And stubborn. It might be easier to go along with her assumptions."

The front door opened before Cali had a chance to argue. She gathered her composure, and turned to the thin, elderly woman who stood at the door, leaning on a cane.

"Well, my lands! You've finally brought over a nice girl for me to meet, Sheriff!" The woman shuffled back, waving them inside. She mumbled under her breath, "It's about time."

Cali glanced at Nick in time to see him shrug, and mouth a silent, "I told you so."

She hid a grin and followed Nick inside, catching the tempting aroma of something sweet baking in the kitchen. The woman turned her hazel eyes to Cali. "I don't believe we've met before. I'm Mrs. Mayes."

"Cali Stevens."

"Oh, dear. I should've recognized you. You're that friend of the missing girl aren't you? I saw you up there on TV." She waved a hand at the small television set in her living room. "I'm so sorry. You never know what people are thinking these days do you?" She placed a well-worn hand on Cali's shoulder and patted her. She looked at Nick. "You find that missing girl, and when you catch the scoundrel who took her, you string him up by his toes and whup him!"

Cali bit her cheek to keep from smiling at the woman's passionate words. "I'd like to see that, Mrs. Mayes."

Nick stood straighter and stepped forward, appearing every part the dutiful sheriff. "Now, Mrs. Mayes. You know we have a justice system that takes care of the criminals we catch. We aren't allowed to string up anyone by their toes."

Cali had no idea how Nick had said those words with a straight face. But he had.

"But wouldn't you like to? Just once?" Mrs. Mayes prodded.

His stern expression collapsed and he broke into a grin. "The thought has occurred to me a time or two."

"I knew it." Mrs. Mayes turned to make her way into the kitchen, but not before Cali caught the triumphant smile growing on her face. "Follow me. I have a cherry cobbler cooking. It should be about done now."

Cali stepped into the brightly decorated kitchen with Nick right behind her. He placed his hand on her lower back and pulled a chair out at the table, and a tingling warmth spread up her spine. She wondered if Nick was being thoughtful again, or if he only wanted to play along with Mrs. Mayes's matchmaking attempts. Either way, she liked how it felt to have someone looking out for her. Not someone, she corrected. Nick.

Mrs. Mayes opened a cupboard for a set of plates.

"I'll get those for you." Nick stepped over to help. He grabbed three small plates and set them on the table. Before Mrs. Mayes had a chance to take out the cobbler, he found an oven mitt and opened the door.

"You'll make someone a fine husband one day, Nick. Course, I've been telling you that a long time. Are you married Ms. Stevens?"

Cali felt a full-blown blush heat her face. Nick plopped the cobbler on the stove and turned to face her. His mouth twitched into a grin.

"No ma'am."

"Been courting anyone as of late?"

She hadn't heard the term "courting" since her grandmother had used it years ago. "Um, I, no ma'am, I'm not dating anyone."

Nick took the initiative to save her from further questions. "Have a seat, Mrs. Mayes. I'll serve the cobbler, then get to that leaky faucet you need repaired."

"You're such a dear." She scooted into a chair and set aside her cane, looking relieved to sit. "My George used to take care of the maintenance. The good Lord took him home eight years ago as of last month. I still miss him to this day." She looked at the portion Nick set out on each of the plates. "Get more, Nick. You need to keep your strength up to catch that stalker dude."

Cali choked on her first bite of cobbler. "Stalker dude?"

Mrs. Mayes cupped her hand to her cheek, as if to hide her answer from Nick. "My grandson keeps me up to date on all of the new terms the kids are using these days."

Cali had to smother another grin. "Do you see him often?"

"No, he lives in Washington State. But he sends me e-mails all the time. Nick here is the one who looks after me now. I don't know what I'd do without him." Mrs. Mayes patted his arm and took a bite of cobbler. After swallowing she added, "Of course, I keep telling him he should have better things to do with his time than hang out with an old lady."

Nick put an arm around Mrs. Mayes and tugged her close. "Now, Mrs. Mayes, you know I can't resist being in the company of such a lovely woman." He planted a quick kiss on her cheek.

Mrs. Mayes hid her mouth with a napkin as she giggled. "If only I were forty years younger." She sighed, leaning her head on his shoulder and resting her hand over her heart.

Cali laughed at the woman's theatrical flirtation.

Mrs. Mayes looked at Cali and added, "You know, he's turned away every woman I've tossed his way. And let me tell you, there have been plenty of them. He's a finicky one, I guarantee you that."

Cali's interest piqued and she turned her gaze to Nick.

"It's not that I don't appreciate your help, Mrs. Mayes." Nick pulled his arm back, sat straight and took another mouthful of cobbler, finishing his plate.

When he didn't give more information, Mrs. Mayes offered, "There's more cobbler if you'd like."

"I couldn't eat another bite. Thanks."

Disappointment hit Cali. She had hoped Nick would explain why he had turned away the women.

Mrs. Mayes sighed. "My George used to say he couldn't eat another bite. Then after an hour I'd catch him sneaking another plateful." Her smile faded and she admitted, "You know, it gets lonely around here sometimes. Everyone needs somebody." Then she squared her shoulders, lifted her chin and added, "Right Nick?" She nudged him with her elbow.

He cleared his throat and gathered the dishes. "I'll get to that faucet now. You said it's the one in the bathtub?"

"That's right. Every night I hear drip...drip...drop. It darn near drives me crazy. I can't sleep 'cause of it. Last night I tried stuffing a washcloth under the drip."

"Did it work?" Cali asked.

"Nope. All it did was change the sound to a smack...smack...smack. I considered taking a hammer to the faucet, but remembered Nick had promised to come by, so I didn't."

Cali chuckled, liking the spirited woman more each minute they spent together.

Nick said, "I'll take care of it for you. I'll go get my tools from the truck."

When he stepped outside, the screen door slapped shut behind him and Mrs. Mayes immediately spoke up. "You should know you're the first girl he's brought over here for me to meet."

Although tempted to explain the real reason Nick had brought her here, Cali played along. "Is that right?"

"Yes. He's a good man."

"I've been told that before." She remembered Helen's kind words about Nick. *Honest. Trustworthy.* But, could she trust him to find Serena?

"He likes you."

Cali shook her head. "He feels responsible for me."

"Maybe so. But, take it from someone who's been around the block a few times, he likes you."

She warmed at the woman's hopeful expression. "I like him, too."

"I think he's handsome, and a good catch."

"I do, too."

Mrs. Mayes slammed her fist on the table. "Ha! I knew it." A gloating smile beamed on her thin lips.

"Knew what?" Nick asked from behind.

Cali wanted to slink under the table and hide, but she settled for shifting lower in her seat.

Mrs. Mayes looked at the ceiling, then at the walls. Her gaze finally landed on the table, and she wiped a few crumbs from the lacey tablecloth. "It's nothing, dear. Just girl talk."

"I see. If you don't tell me now, Mrs. Mayes, I'll get it out of Cali later. Apparently, I have a certain finesse that makes it hard for people to resist answering my questions."

"You go on ahead and interrogate her later. I'm

sure she wouldn't mind."

Cali sucked in a breath and sank lower in her seat.

"Mrs. Mayes..." Nick scolded.

"What?" she asked innocently.

Cali would have argued, but knew deep down the woman was right. She liked Nick, more and more each day and she wouldn't mind spending time alone with him. The realization struck her, and she bolted from the chair. "I see you have a lovely view of the bay. Mind if I take a peek outside?" She pretended to see a bit of the view from the kitchen window.

"Certainly. I'll join you."

Cali caught the grin on Nick's face before he turned and headed to the bathroom. Mrs. Mayes stepped outside on the porch, using her cane for support, and Cali followed, trying to hide her intense reaction to Mrs. Mayes's matchmaking attempts.

As they settled into a pair of pastel colored Adirondack chairs, Mrs. Mayes commented, "You said Nick feels responsible for you."

"Yes, he does."

"That's not a bad thing you know."

"I've always taken care of myself. I can handle..."

"Ah. I see."

When she became quiet, Cali looked over at her. In the sunlight, Mrs. Mayes's appearance took on a healthy, natural glow. Her wrinkles added to her charm, rather than taking away from it. Mrs. Mayes sat, picking imaginary fluff from her purple, cotton dress, as if debating what to say next.

"What do you see?" Cali prodded.

"I see your fear. You know, letting someone help you...take care of you doesn't mean you're not a strong person. Sometimes God puts people into our lives to help us. And it's up to us to accept that help."

"I can handle..."

"Maybe you can. But should you?"

Taken aback, Cali sat still for a moment. "I guess I've always been afraid if I follow someone else's lead I'll be giving up control. That scares me."

"We aren't in control anyway."

Cali laughed. "That's what Nick told me."

"He's a smart man. Maybe he learned it from me. I was his Sunday school teacher for years you know."

"I didn't know."

"It's true. I've known him since he was born. He comes from a fine family, and he's turned into a fine man. He's found the niche God planned for him. He feels responsible to you, and this whole island of people, not out of his official duty, but from his passion for life and from his passion for serving Christ. Even if he wasn't the sheriff, Nick would still want to look out for you. It's who he is."

"I admire that."

Nick walked around the corner of the cottage, startling Cali. "Admire what?"

"You," Cali answered without thinking. A shot of heat ran directly to her cheeks.

His eyebrows lifted and a smile spread across his face as he strode up to lean his elbows across the white porch railing. "Is that so?"

"It is."

"I admire you too, Cali."

His gaze locked onto hers, and her breathing hitched and then stopped altogether.

"Do I hear my cell phone ringing?" Mrs. Mayes stood and headed inside. Cali didn't hear a thing besides the blood rushing through her ears.

Nick stepped onto the porch and took the seat next to her. "Mrs. Mayes is quite a character, isn't she?"

"Yes, she is. Did you fix the faucet?" Cali answered, searching for a change of subject, hoping the flush in her cheeks would drain away.

"Yep. It only took a minute." His gaze followed a sailboat slowly passing by on the bay.

"How often do you come here?"

"At least once a week, sometimes more around the holidays."

"Do her sons come to visit much?"

He shrugged. "Every so often. But, not as often as she'd like them to."

Cali shifted in her seat. "She must get lonely."

He focused on her and his voice softened, "I do what I can…"

"You do more than most people would."

"Yeah, well, I'm not most people."

Cali agreed, but didn't dare say it. In the short time she had known him, he had more than earned her respect and admiration. As her knowledge of him grew, so did her attraction.

Nick studied her as if her thoughts were transparent. She knew her blush returned when she felt a fresh wave of heat crawling up her cheeks. She quickly looked away, shifting her feet as if she needed to reposition.

Nick shifted too, and cleared his throat. "Ready to go?"

"Whenever you are."

He stood and offered his hand. "Mind if we stop by the station on the way to my place? I need to check on a few things."

"That's fine." Cali placed her hand in his and let him pull her to her feet. He stepped to open the door, and she felt his gaze follow her into the cottage, causing her nerve endings to tingle. He stepped in behind her and cupped her shoulders in his hands, stopping her before she made it to the kitchen. He leaned in close behind her, and his warm breath touched her ear as he whispered, "You'd better get rid of that blush before Mrs. Mayes sees you, or she'll think her matchmaking attempts have already worked. You look radiant, Cali."

Chapter Fourteen

You look radiant. Nick's whispered words echoed in Cali's mind as he drove the truck through the winding roads leading to the station. She glanced repeatedly in his direction as they rode in silence, but his features didn't betray his thoughts. Her rapid pulse finally slowed by the time he parked the truck.

"This shouldn't take too long. Then I'll take you home."

Cali's heart lodged in her throat. Nick meant *his* home. She scrambled from the truck before he had a chance to help her out. She knew if he touched her hand again, he would send her pulse on another run.

Nick held the door for her as they entered the station. Helen stood behind the desk, shuffling through papers, and Deputy Owen stood nearby sipping a cup of steaming coffee. Another deputy whom Cali didn't recognize walked down the hallway toward the cells in the back.

Owen looked up. "Sheriff. Cali." He nodded a greeting and ambled over to them.

Every trace of softness in Nick's voice vanished when he said, "I want to see the pictures."

Helen looked up from her paperwork. "I put

them on your desk, Sheriff."

Nick looked at Cali as if unsure of what to do with her. She solved his dilemma by walking over to speak with Helen. "No coffee cake today?"

Cali caught Nick's movements from the corner of her eye as he walked with Deputy Owen into his office and shut the door.

Helen smiled, but lacked the warmth she had shown before. "Not today." Dark circles of fatigue lay under her eyes.

Apprehension settled over Cali, and her muscles tensed. "What's wrong? Has something happened?"

Helen sighed. "No. That's the problem. We need to find the stalker, Cali. The phone's been ringing off the hook ever since the sheriff's press conference. The stalker has every woman on the island running scared."

The phone rang.

Helen answered it. "Yes ma'am. We are doing everything possible." She paused. "We are taking this seriously. Lower your voice ma'am. The sheriff is..." She blew out a breath and replaced the handset. Apparently, the caller had hung up.

"I wish I could help you," Cali offered.

Helen waved Cali's concern away. "It ain't nothing I can't handle. Oh, I almost forgot. I got a call for you earlier today," she said before the phone rang again. She answered it, leaving Cali wondering who could have possibly called for her at the sheriff's station.

Deputy Owen stepped out of Nick's office saying, "I'll go check right now." His watchful eyes settled on Cali, and he acknowledged her with a nod before walking outside to his cruiser. She watched him back out of his parking spot, wondering what lead they may have found.

Helen said, "Hold on a minute please." She put the caller on hold and handed Cali a square slip of paper. "A woman called asking for you. She wouldn't leave her name. Only her number. Said for you to call her." She picked up the handset again and took the waiting caller off hold.

Cali looked at the number written on the note. The first three digits belonged to Coral Isle's area code. She didn't recognize the last seven digits, and her pulse kicked up a notch. *Who could have called*?

"Dear Lord, it couldn't be Serena, could it?" Her heart slammed into her chest, and she felt dizzy. She reached for her cell phone, but remembered she had left her purse in Nick's truck.

Cali hurried over to his office and nearly collided with him as he came out. He grasped her arms to steady her. "Is everything all right?"

"I need to use your phone," she said sounding breathless.

"Go ahead. I'll be right back." If he noticed her anxiety, he didn't comment on it before leaving her alone in the office.

Cali walked to the desk and sat in Nick's leather chair, comforted by the warmth he had left behind. She picked up the phone with shaky hands, and prayed as she dialed the number, *Lord, please let it be her. Let her be OK*. But as she said the prayer, her common sense overcame her hope. If it had been Serena, she would have identified herself.

A woman's gravelly voice answered on the third ring, "Hello?"

"I'm Cali Stevens. I got a message…"

"Where are you?" The voice sounded deep for a woman, and unusually raspy.

"Who is this?"

"I'm the first victim."

Cali stopped breathing. Seconds ticked by before she found her voice. "What's your name?"

"Nancy." She sucked in a breath and blew it out, sounding as if she were taking a drag on a cigarette.

"Why did you call me?"

The woman snorted. "I thought you might like to

know what kind of twisted jerk has your friend held captive. But if you don't…"

"No, wait! Don't hang up. What can you tell me?"

"Not a whole lot. But nothing over the phone. I'll tell you what I can in person."

The hairs on Cali's neck stood on end and her palms dampened. "Why can't you tell me now?"

"Do you want to talk or not?"

"Yes, of course."

"I'll meet you on the beach at the Half Shell Road public access in an hour."

Cali glanced at her watch. "An hour? I don't know if I can…" The dial tone sounded in her ear. She looked at the note. Realizing she had not written Nancy's instructions, Cali scribbled the location and the woman's name on the paper.

Cali's mind raced and her anxiety surged in intensity when it occurred to her she did not have a car, which left her under Nick's control. Even if Helen or another deputy agreed to take her, they would seek Nick's approval first. Ultimately, he would decide if she met with the woman or not. The realization paralyzed her with fear. What if he refused?

Cali ran a hand through her hair, and then covered her eyes with her palms as her frustration grew. *Lord, I'm backed into a corner here. I have an opportunity to find out something about Serena, but I'm not in a position to decide whether to go or not. Please help me know what to do.* After a moment, she dropped her hands. Nick stood silently in the doorway, watching her with concern.

She had no choice but to give up control and trust someone. Someone God had put in her life for a reason. "I trust you to make the right decision, Nick."

Confusion crossed his features but he remained motionless.

"I need you." She stood and crossed the room, stopping a few feet from him.

He stepped into the office and shut the door. "I'm here for you, Cali."

"You know it's hard for me to rely on someone else. But I'm learning a little at a time that God wants me to rely on Him, and on...you." She looked away from his probing gaze, feeling much as she had when she'd walked into his office the first time.

Fearful. Anxious. At his mercy.

"What is it?" Nick cupped her face, turning it.

"The stalker's first victim called earlier looking for me." She covered his hand with hers. "I called her back. She wants to talk. She told me the place where she's going to be in an hour. Nick, I need you to take me to her."

He stiffened and dropped his hand. "How do you know it was really her?"

"She said her name was Nancy."

"Nancy Chandler," he paused. "I've already obtained detailed statements from her. What else could she have to say to you that she didn't already tell me?" He crossed his arms and studied her as if she had all the answers.

"I don't know. Maybe she's remembered something since she talked to you. I think it's worth checking out."

He rubbed his hand across his jaw and blew out a deep breath.

"Please, Nick." Cali cringed at the desperation in her voice. Her heart drummed hard against her chest as she waited for his reply.

"I've been telling you to stay out of the investigation since we met. What makes you think I'd willingly take you right into the middle of it now?"

She shrugged and dropped her voice into a whisper. "Because I'm not a stranger anymore."

He shook his head and rested his hands on his

hips. "That's even more reason for me to want to keep you out of it. I care about you Cali. I don't want anything happening to you."

"You'll be right there. What can happen?"

When Nick remained silent, she added, "I want to help. I need to do something. I cannot stand on the sidelines and watch. I need to be a part of this. Serena means so much to me."

His features softened as his gaze swept over her. "Cali…"

She took a hesitant step closer and sucked in a shaky breath. "You've been telling me I'm not in control…that I try to carry too much load on my shoulders. I'm willing to give up that load, and I'm willing to trust you. It's your choice, Nick, and I trust you to make the right one."

Nick looked into the clear-blue depths of Cali's eyes and saw the truth. She meant what she said. A sense of satisfaction swept over him, knowing he had gotten through to her. But the pressure of the decision lay heavily on his shoulders. He wanted to keep Cali as safe as possible, and allowing her deeper into the investigation could be dangerous. However, Nancy Chandler must have called for a reason.

The intercom crackled. "Sheriff. Deputy Owen is calling for you."

Glancing at the intercom, Nick stepped to it and pressed the button. "Put him through, Helen," he said, glad for the temporary interruption.

"I'll wait outside." Cali started to leave.

"No. Stay here. It'll only take a minute." The call came through and he answered it, not bothering to sit. "Justice."

"It's a dead end."

"Are you sure?"

"Positive."

He sighed and ran a hand through his hair. "Come on back in." He hung up. Another possible lead had ended up nowhere, leaving very few options. Maybe it wouldn't be a bad idea to let Cali talk to the victim after all.

Decision made, he looked at her and said, "All right. I'll take you. But..."

Before he finished his sentence, she surprised him by springing into his arms. "Thank you, Nick."

There she was with her arms wrapped around his waist, pressing against him again, and he knew within a split second he was going to kiss her.

He should keep her at a distance to protect her, and to keep her from becoming a distraction. But, at this point, no amount of common sense could change his mind. He set his reservations aside and wrapped an arm around her, keeping her from drawing away. He cupped a hand on the nape of her neck, and tilted her head, bringing her lips close. Surprise registered on her face, and she gasped right before he brought his mouth to hers and felt the soft dampness of her lips pressed against his. He teased her lips apart, taking more of what he'd wanted since he first met her. He took his time, caressing her mouth. She leaned into him, and her skin heated beneath his touch.

He released her lips and placed feathery kisses on her forehead, her temple, and her cheek. He dipped his head, catching the light fragrance of roses in her hair, on her skin.

He didn't want to let her go, but knew he had to.

When he drew away, her eyes had turned a shade darker, reminding him of the storm-tossed sea. He took a full step back, enjoying the fresh blush spreading across her features.

"I didn't see that coming," her voice wavered as she looked away and smoothed her hair.

"I'll be sure to warn you next time."

Her blush deepened and her gaze darted around the office. Nick grinned, satisfied he had stirred her as much as she had stirred him.

A knock sounded at his door, making Cali jump. She stepped back as a guilty expression crossed her face. Nick sobered instantly. Guilt was the last thing he wanted her to feel as a result of his kiss.

Nick reminded himself where he was, and what he should be doing. "Come in." His voice sounded raspy, and he wished he had cleared his throat before speaking. He straightened and watched the door.

Helen peeked through. "Here's a copy of the report you asked for." She walked in and handed the folder to him, assessing him first, and then Cali with her gaze. "It is a little warm in here, Sheriff. I'll set the air-conditioner lower." The hint of a knowing smile tugged at the corner of her lips, and her eyes sparkled. Nick assumed Helen had noticed the blush on both of their faces.

"Good idea," he agreed.

Helen stepped out, closing the door as she walked away. Apparently, Mrs. Mayes wasn't the only one who had decided he should have a woman in his life. Nick's thoughts strayed to Cali, along with his gaze. He swallowed as his heart continued to race. The more time he spent with Cali, the more he began to think Mrs. Mayes and Helen could be right.

Focusing back on the office, Nick stepped to the desk and placed the report on top of a neatly stacked pile, then picked up the note Cali had left beside the telephone. "Half Shell Road. We'd better get going or we'll be late." He started for the door, but at the last second stopped to pick up the pictures Helen had snapped at the press conference.

Cali looked at him with a question in her eyes, and the glimmer of hope she always carried with her.

He shook his head. "Don't get your hopes up. We didn't find anything unusual in the pictures."

"I'd still like to see them."

"Later. We have to get to the beach. Nancy Chandler isn't the type of woman who likes to be kept waiting."

Chapter Fifteen

Cali found Nancy Chandler before Nick had a chance to point her out. She held a long, thin cigarette in her mouth as she sat alone at the edge of a sand dune with her knees drawn, and her chin held high. She peered out over the ocean, and appeared to be lost in thought.

Her lips formed a thin line, which parted to take a drag on the cigarette. Slivers of gray streaked her mousy brown hair, which she had pulled back into a severe bun at the base of her neck. Her long, beak-like nose jutted out farther than her sunken chin. Hostility manifested in her narrow, jade-colored eyes, as she glanced over and spotted Nick.

"I didn't say anything about bringing the law with you," her raspy voice grated as she turned her focus on Cali.

"Nick only wants to help."

"Nick is it?" Nancy's eyebrows lifted.

Cali straightened her spine. "Yes. Nick."

"Well, I didn't call *Nick*, did I?"

Cali looked at Nick, about to defend him, but he held his hands up in surrender. "I'll be down at the water." He met Cali's eyes briefly before turning and walking away.

Her focus returned to the woman, and she couldn't help but wonder why the stalker had picked such a rude, unattractive person as a target.

"Not what you thought I'd look like, huh?" Nancy asked as if she read Cali's thoughts.

"You're not what I expected."

"Who knows why the guy picked me." She took a long puff on her cigarette and shifted her gaze to Cali, letting out a low humorless laugh. "I know I'm not the most attractive woman on the island, but I don't think that's what matters to him."

Cali's interest peaked. "What do you mean?" She positioned herself in the sand a few feet away.

Nancy shook her head. "I…" her voice trailed off. She stared at the sea for a few moments. Her cigarette burned to the filter and she snuffed it out in the sand. She immediately lit another. "Care for a cancer stick?" Nancy held up her pack of cigarettes.

"No." Cali's patience had already worn thin. "What makes you say attraction doesn't matter to him?"

Nancy blew out a deep, smoke-filled breath. "The way he looked at me."

"You saw what he looked like?"

"Not his face. But I did see his eyes through his mask. Dark, evil eyes." A deep shiver passed through the hardened woman.

Cali felt a pang of sympathy break through. "I'm sorry this happened to you."

Nancy shook her head. "You don't even know what happened. How can you be sorry?"

"Then tell me."

"I have memories. Fuzzy flashbacks. I don't know which are dreams and which are reality. He kept me drugged. At least that's what the sheriff believes happened. I don't know exactly. All I know is two weeks of my life are now mostly a horrifying blur."

Nick stood at the shoreline as Cali waited for more details from Nancy. He occasionally glanced at them, before returning his focus to the crashing surf.

Cali slid her feet deeper into the sand, completely covering them, as questions tumbled through her mind.

"I shouldn't have called you." Nancy started to rise.

"No wait!" Confusion reeled through her. "You wanted me to know something. What was it?"

Nancy hesitated. "I told the sheriff everything I can remember." She stood, crossing her arms.

"You're shivering. Is there something you don't want to tell him? Something personal?" She rose to stand beside Nancy. "Then tell me. Maybe I can help."

"You think you know it all? You think you can waltz right in and solve my problems?"

"You called me. Remember?" A rush of anger surfaced. "If you want to tell me something, do it. Otherwise, stop wasting my time."

A smile spread across the woman's lips. "Yes, I did call you. And now, I'm not disappointed. I watched the press conference. I saw your determination."

"And?"

"And I wanted to see you in person. I wanted to know if you have what it takes to do something."

"What do you mean?"

"This island needs someone like you."

"Me?"

"You. You're a reporter aren't you? Write some articles." Nancy waved her hand, her cigarette sending spirals of smoke into the air. "Start a program. I don't know." Tears welled in her eyes, before she quickly swiped them away. "People need to know such evil exists, even in paradise. The man who took me. He's strong. He's obsessive. And, he could be anyone." She fanned her hands out. "Absolutely anyone."

Cali recognized fear in Nancy's eyes and her defenses softened.

"I can understand you wanting to find your friend. But just remember, when Serena is released, he'll still be out there. Waiting. Watching for more victims."

"Nick's going to catch him," Cali said with confidence.

"Eventually. But what happens until then? What if that monster stays on the streets long enough to kidnap another woman? What about the other criminals out there preying on innocent people? You can help, Cali. Use your determination and your skills as a reporter to make people aware of the dangers."

"This isn't what I expected."

"I know what you expected. I told you I know what kind of man has Serena. And I will tell you. But, promise me you'll consider helping to raise awareness."

Desperation entered Nancy's gaze, something Cali would not have thought possible a few minutes ago. Her voice softened as she saw through the woman's tough exterior. "I'll see what I can do."

"I suppose that's all I can ask." Nancy ground out her cigarette before stuffing the remnants into her pocket. "Now, about the guy who took me. I have a hunch about him."

"A hunch?"

"Yeah. But, you won't find it in the official reports." She sighed. "The sheriff wants evidence, not intuition."

"You can tell Nick anything. He would listen."

A glimmer appeared in Nancy's eyes. "You've got a thing for him?"

Cali didn't respond verbally, but she knew the blush on her face gave her away.

"It's only natural. He is hot." Nancy stated easily, as if revealing a simple fact about the weather.

"About the stalker?" Cali prodded, somewhat

irritated and afraid Nancy would stray from the subject again.

"He's organized. Smart. He wants to have authority. He seemed to thrive by controlling me."

"You didn't tell the sheriff this?"

"Yeah, I did. But I didn't tell him I think the stalker's from the island."

"What makes you think he lives here? A hunch?"

"Something like that."

"If there's something you're not saying..."

"I recall smelling alcohol on him a time or two. I didn't mention it because I'm not positive about it."

"Is there anything else?"

Nancy blew out a breath. "No."

"You should've told Nick about the alcohol. He may be hanging around bars. Looking for more victims."

"Yeah, well, smelling Piña Coladas and Margaritas in a vacation community isn't that rare, you know."

"He should know," Cali insisted.

Nancy stepped back. "You tell him. I'm outta here." She turned and headed toward the pathway leading to the parking lot.

Cali discovered the reason for Nancy's abrupt departure. Nick was approaching.

"I gather she's done talking," he said as he walked to Cali. "I get the feeling she doesn't like me."

"She might not like you, but at least she thinks you're cute." Cali couldn't bring herself to say the word *hot*, because that's exactly what she was thinking as he stood beside her with his broad shoulders outlined by his snug fitting T-shirt, and his deep-blue eyes drawing her in. She had to be careful, or she might get caught staring again.

"Is that so?" His mouth curved into a slight smile. "I never would've guessed."

His arm brushed hers and a jolt of awareness

shot through her. She inched closer as she remembered how secure she felt in his arms, and how enticing his lips had tasted.

"So, what did she say?"

Nick stared at her expectantly. Embarrassed at how he so easily distracted her, and without even trying, she looked away. "There are a few things you might find interesting. But, let's get out of this heat first."

"Good idea." He splayed his hand at the small of her back as they began walking. She liked the warmth of his touch, and the gentle pressure as he guided her to the truck. She replayed Nancy's words in her mind, trying to remember everything she had said, and trying to stay focused on the reason for the meeting.

Nick opened the truck's passenger side door, and Cali climbed in and waited for him to settle in his seat. He buckled his seatbelt before she asked, "Do you think the stalker could be from the island?"

"It's possible." He started the engine and pulled out onto the road. "We should know more when the FBI profilers send their report."

"Nancy thinks he's from here."

Nick directed his sharp gaze at her. "Why?"

"Intuition?" Cali shrugged. "I don't know. She called it a hunch."

"Mmm. Anything else I should know about?"

"She said she thought she smelled alcohol on him a few times. Maybe he goes to bars to scout out women."

"Not necessarily. Alcohol is available at a lot of places."

"But..."

"And, so far, the victims have said they never went to any bars. You said yourself Serena never goes to them."

She remembered telling Deputy Owen that in the initial report. Her hopes sank. "I just want something to hold on to. Some sort of hope. A lead. Something."

"We'll find her, Cali."

"I know. I'd just like to find her sooner rather than later."

"Did Nancy tell you anything else?"

"Nothing important. No wait, she did mention she thought I should consider writing articles..."

He straightened. Raising his voice he said, "No. No more articles. The newspapers are feeding this guy's ego. The more publicity he gets, the happier he is."

"But you gave the press conference..."

"I gave the conference to ask for help in locating Serena. The press needs to focus on her, but instead they're grinding out wild theories about the stalker." His hands gripped the wheel tighter. "Which puts him in the spotlight." He shook his head. "It's not what I was striving for."

Cali had intended to tell Nick about Nancy's idea about writing public awareness articles, but seeing how upset he became at the mention of newspaper articles in general, she let the subject drop. "Are we heading to your cottage now?"

"Yep. It's time to get you settled in."

Ready for a chance to rest, and to think about all that had happened since she had arrived at Coral Isle, the idea of settling in should have provided a sense of relief. However, thinking of settling in on the upper floor of Nick's cottage twisted her stomach in knots.

Cali wondered if his home would be as well-organized and no-nonsense as his office. She also wondered if she would feel comfortable staying so near to him. One thing was certain; she was about to find out.

Chapter Sixteen

Cali's anticipation intensified when Nick's oceanfront cottage came into view. The two-story home stood above the ground on stilts, like many other cottages near the ocean's edge. The quaint cottage looked like paradise compared to the Sea Urchin. A rainbow-colored wind catcher twirled near the mailbox, and various potted plants and flowers peeked over the edge of the porches above.

Nick pulled into the driveway, parking next to her car.

"My car's already here."

"I asked Deputies Owen and Castle to bring it over before their shift ended."

"I appreciate it. Thank them for me next time you talk to them."

"I will."

He turned off the truck's engine and removed the keys. "I hope you like it here. A cleaning service comes every week after the renters leave, so it should be clean for you." He fiddled with his keys, making him appear nervous, as if he cared what she thought of his home.

"I'm sure it will be fine." Cali stepped out, excited to learn more about Nick's personal life. "I appreciate you taking me in."

"No problem."

She started to open the truck's back door where they had placed her luggage.

"I'll get it." Nick reached around, catching the handle before she could. She turned to face him and his arm brushed hers, sending sparks of awareness through her. He had trapped her between him and the vehicle. He was close. Close enough to kiss her again. She remembered the feel of his solid muscles as he had held her in his embrace. She remembered how secure she had felt. Her legs weakened, and her gaze traveled to his lips.

"Cali."

"Hmm?" She drew her gaze to his.

"I need room to open the door."

Waves of heat bombarded her. "Sorry." She stepped to the side.

Grinning, he pulled out her duffle bag and slung it over his shoulder. Taking her suitcase in his other hand, his gaze met hers and held.

Moments later, Cali realized she was staring again. She removed her laptop and pillow from the backseat, feeling Nick's gaze trailing each of her movements. She stepped back to allow him to shut the door.

"Have dinner with me."

Her breathing hitched. Her heartbeat quickened. Was he asking her on a date? She hugged her pillow, glad she had something to hide the pulse at the base of her neck. "I'd love to."

He flashed a smile. "I'll have it ready by the time you get settled."

She lifted her brows. "You're cooking?"

"Yeah. You'd be amazed at all the things I can do that aren't directly related to my job."

The reply caught her off guard. She pondered her response as he led her up two flights of porch steps. Arriving at the upper level of the cottage, she said, "I suppose some people see the uniform and only think of you as an officer, don't they?"

He stopped to look at her. "Most people do."
"That must be hard."
He shrugged. "It depends on who it is." His gaze flickered over her before he set down her suitcase and slid his key into the sliding glass door. "If it's someone I'd like to know on a personal level, I'd much rather them see me, than the uniform."

She had stopped thinking of him as an officer the night he had rescued her on the beach after the press conference. It seemed like a long time ago, even though it had only been yesterday. "I see the man behind the uniform." *And I like what I see,* she thought, but didn't dare speak the words aloud.

Nick shot a smile in her direction and opened the door. They stepped inside, and he set the key on an end table. The cloudy sky shielded the sunlight from brightening the room, and he switched on a tall lamp beside the sofa. The room lit up, showing a comfortably furnished rental home.

"There are two bedrooms and one bathroom down the hall. The kitchen is small, but it has everything you need," he paused, "except food." He walked to a back room and came out a moment later without her luggage.

Is that why he had offered to make dinner? Unsure of the reason behind his offer, she said, "I can run to the store tonight if you'd rather not cook."

He stepped close and lowered his voice. "I want to."

"If you're sure. I don't want to be a burden..."

"Cali?"

"Yeah?"

He brushed a few strands of hair from her face. "I'm sure." His fingers left a trail of heat in their wake. "Make yourself at home. Come on down when you're ready."

She managed a smile. "Thanks Nick. I will."

He left her standing in the living room with a warm thrill of excitement coursing through her veins. Nick Justice, Sheriff of Coral Isle, had invited her into his home to protect her, and had offered to make her dinner. Cali's heart beat wild in her chest and she blew out a breath to calm her nerves.

She sank into the sofa. Knowing he was downstairs provided a welcoming sense of security, and she found herself beginning to relax for the first time in days.

Her cell phone rang, disrupting the quiet room, and she checked the caller ID. Cali flipped the phone open. "Hey, Dad."

"Just calling to see what's going on over on the coast." His familiar voice sent another wave of security her way.

"No word on Serena yet. But, I have moved out of the old motel."

"Moved? Where? Why?"

"I'm staying on the upper floor of Nick's cottage. He usually rents it out to tourists. Maybe I should offer to pay him," she said as the thought struck her. She avoided the 'why' question altogether.

"I think you'd insult him if you offered to pay him."

"Why do you say that?"

"Because I got the feeling from talking with him on the phone, that he takes his job seriously."

"He does. But..."

"And that includes looking after you."

"He does have a strong protective streak in him. He's thoughtful too. He knows I don't have any food, so he's offered to make dinner."

"Dinner? Maybe there's more to his intentions than his duty to protect and serve?"

"It's just dinner," she said, although it felt like much more than that.

"Uh huh."

"So, how's Mom?" Cali asked in a light tone, trying to bounce subjects.

"Nice try. Tell me more about this sheriff you

seem so fond of."

"I...he..." Cali sighed, knowing her feelings for Nick went far beyond a few words of description. "He's looking out for me. He's a good guy. You'd like him."

"We'll see. If he's willing and able to keep you safe, he has my approval."

Cali already felt safer with Nick close by. She remembered how terrified she had felt waking up alone in the motel room and discovering the stalker had been there, and was glad Nick had insisted on bringing her home. She debated whether to tell her dad about the incident, but thought it would only cause him to worry.

"How are things at the *Herald*?"

"We're surviving."

Guilt tugged at her. "I'm sorry to leave for so long. I know you wanted the article about the upcoming Brookstone festival to be ready by this weekend. I feel like I've left you hanging."

"Don't worry about it. We miss you, but we're managing just fine."

"I wish I could be at two places at once."

He chuckled. "Don't we all?"

"I'd better go so I can offer to help with dinner."

"OK, hon'. Stay safe."

As usual, he disconnected without saying goodbye.

Cali grabbed the key from the end table, and headed for the glass door. She reached for the handle, and then stopped, debating whether to refresh her lipstick and brush her hair before going downstairs.

"It's not a real date," she assured herself. But, she caught her blush in the mirror as she remembered the promise Nick had given her after he had kissed her. *I'll be sure to warn you next time.*

Next time.

Cali's blush deepened as she wondered when

that would be. Guilt washed over her. Then regret stabbed at her. Serena had not been found yet. How could she be thinking about starting a relationship when her best friend was still missing?

She shook her head, refused the lipstick and left her hair tangled from the wind. Walking out, she locked the door behind her and lifted her chin. "Stay focused on the search, Cali." Her whispered words worked...for the whole twenty seconds it took to walk downstairs to Nick's level. Then she spotted him through the window.

He had changed clothes. He still wore jeans, but they were a shade darker than he'd had on before. His grey T-shirt clung to what looked like damp skin, and his dark hair glistened with moisture. He must have just showered. Cali's throat dried, and she found it difficult to swallow. She wondered if he smelled as good as he looked.

Nick spotted her from the kitchen, where he stood stirring something in a steaming pot on the stove. A smile parted his lips, and he set the ladle on the counter, and then moved to slide the door open. She had her answer. He did smell as good as he looked. The fresh scent of soap clung to his skin, and his lightly scented cologne worked magic.

Cali felt lightheaded, and it was not out of fear this time. "Smells good."

"Thanks. Spaghetti's my specialty."

If only he knew she wasn't talking about the food.

Chapter Seventeen

Cali wished she had put on lipstick after all. She waited until Nick stepped aside and let her into the room before finger combing her hair. "The wind's picking up," she said smoothing her unruly waves.

"The storm's strengthening." He tossed the words over his broad shoulders as he headed back into the kitchen.

His bare feet padded across the floor, and her gaze followed. Her defenses melted away in the casual environment, and a grin spread across her face. She closed the door behind her and ambled into the room. "Can I help?"

"I've got it covered. Do you like garlic on your bread?" Looking up, his gaze darted to her lips. "You should smile more often. It looks good on you."

"I usually do." Her smile faded. "It's been a hard week."

"I know it has." Compassion lined his features. He picked up a table knife and dipped it in butter. He began spreading it on a slice of French bread, his hands moving with precision as he worked. Strong, capable hands.

"Garlic?" he asked again as he picked up the spice container.

Shaken out of her thoughts she answered, "Yes. Please."

Nick carefully covered the piece of bread with sprinkles of garlic. "Make yourself comfortable. It'll be ready soon." He set the bread in the pan and picked up another.

"Are you sure I can't do something? I'm not used to standing back and watching others work."

He set the bread on the counter. Looking at her thoughtfully, he said, "You've done all you can. I have a team of deputies actively working on the case. The FBI is developing a criminal profile. The DNA samples collected from the victims are being processed. So," he shrugged, "you can stop feeling guilty."

"I...I was just talking about dinner."

"Were you?" He picked up the bread again and continued to butter it.

Wasn't she? The day's events began to wear on her, and fatigue weighed her down. Too tired to think about his question, Cali turned and perused the room.

As she had imagined, Nick had only the essentials in the spacious living area. A beige leather sofa and recliner were positioned in front of the stone fireplace. The large, maroon area rug made the room feel cozy and lived in, and a flat-screened television hung mounted on the wall above the mantel, as if it were a family picture to be admired.

Cali didn't want to be invasive, or appear curious, but he had an interesting assortment of items placed on the fireplace mantel, and she could not help but to wander over to it. Cali touched an amber-colored, crackled glass vase, which began the row of glass objects lining the solid oak piece. An oval shaped bowl sat next to it, and a ruby-colored flask sat to the right of the bowl.

"Those are from West Virginia. They're hand-blown." Nick spoke as he walked up beside her.

"They're beautiful."

"My parents travel a lot. When Mom discovered

the company that makes and sells these, she fell in love with them. She's given me one for Christmas for three years in a row."

"You said you were born and raised here. Do your parents still live on the island?"

"Yes. They still live in the cottage I grew up in. But, they aren't home much."

"Where do they go?"

"All over the states. They like to travel, RV style."

"Where are they now?"

"Camping. Probably somewhere around Oregon by now."

Cali's imagination soared. "I'd love to travel. I haven't been very many places outside of Brookstone."

"Why's that?"

She shrugged. "I don't know. I guess I've always been caught up in the family business. I've been working there as long as I can remember."

"By choice?"

Her gaze shot to his. "What do you mean?"

"Working for your father. Is it something you chose, or something that was expected of you?"

She considered his question. "Both. I've always wanted to be a reporter. I practically grew up at the *Herald*, so it was only natural," she paused. "I do admit I've been restless for the past few years."

"Restless?"

"Yes. I can't pinpoint what it is, but I feel like something's missing. I tried changing my writing focus from general events to targeting human-interest stories, hoping the articles would have more of an impact on people's lives. That helped to keep me settled for a while. But, I still feel like I could be doing something more fulfilling. Something with more purpose."

"Maybe God wants to lead you in a new direction."

"Maybe. What about you? How long have you wanted to be in law enforcement?"

"Since kindergarten," he answered without pause.

Cali raised her eyebrows. "That's a long time."

"We had a policeman visit the class one day to talk to us about stranger safety." He rested his hand on the fireplace mantel, and leaned into it. His shirt pulled tight across his broad chest, and Cali had to concentrate to keep track of his words. "He spoke about how it was his job to look out for people and keep them safe. I knew then that was what I wanted to do."

"It's incredible what one person's influence can do, isn't it?"

He tilted his head and his gaze traveled over her face. "It sure is," he said gently.

Cali's pulse quickened as she wondered if there was a deeper meaning behind his words.

His lips broke into a smile. "Besides, I was captivated by his shiny badge and handcuffs."

Cali laughed. "Ahh. The true reason you became a sheriff." She shook her head, smiling.

"You caught me."

She found it hard to concentrate on anything but the humor dancing in his dark-blue eyes. She tore her gaze away. "So, do you have any regrets about becoming an officer?" She took a few steps across the room, running her finger along a row of books lining a tall bookshelf.

Her heart lodged in her throat when she came to the end of the bookshelf and spotted a large bin full of toys. It sat in the corner, wedged up against the wall. A worn, brown teddy bear peeked at her from beneath a toy train, and an assortment of cars, trucks and action figures filled the bin.

Did Nick have a child?

No. It couldn't be. Even as she denied the thought, the possibility reeled through her.

"I can't imagine doing anything else. But, I do regret some of the choices I've made." Nick's words sounded as if they'd come from a far-off distance, although he stood close behind her.

Cali forced herself to breathe, and glanced at him as he rubbed his left shoulder. She scrambled for an appropriate reply. "At least you've learned something from your mistakes."

"Very true."

She wanted to point out the basket full of toys; she wanted to ask if he had a son. But, the questions lodged in her throat. She searched the room, looking for more indications that a child may live here.

A collage picture frame hanging on the wall across the room caught her attention. She walked to it and looked at the assortment of pictures. In one, an older couple stood in front of a large recreational vehicle, hugging each other.

"Are these your parents?"

Nick moved next to her. "Yeah."

"They look happy together."

"They are. Of course, they've had their ups and downs. Raising me and my sister wasn't easy on them. We've both got a strong, stubborn streak in us."

"You have a sister?"

He pointed to another picture with a woman holding a toddler on her hip. "This is Casey, my baby sister. And this little guy is Charlie. He turned five a few weeks ago."

"You have a sister?" she repeated. "And a nephew?"

"A brother-in-law, too."

"Do they live close by?"

"They live on the island. William, her husband, moved from Chicago to be here with her. Casey's always loved it here as much as I do and William knew she wouldn't be happy living anywhere else."

"How did they meet?"

"Casey owns and runs a whale-watching charter boat service. William was vacationing here and signed up for the half-day cruise. Apparently they fell in love at first sight."

"Apparently?"

"Yeah. He never left the island. He bought a cottage, hired a moving company to bring his stuff down from Chicago and married Casey. He's never looked back."

Cali smiled wistfully. "It sounds like it was meant to be."

"They do seem happy together. They had Charlie about a year after they were married."

"So the toys...?" Cali took the opportunity to ask as she motioned to the bin in the corner.

"They're Charlie's. Every time he comes over, he ends up leaving one of the handfuls of toys he brings with him. And I'll admit I've bought him a thing or two to play with while I'm watching him." Nick's eyes lit up as he spoke about his nephew. "I get to spoil him and hand him back to his parents. It's the best part of being an uncle."

Cali released the breath she'd been holding. "So, you don't have kids?"

"Not yet."

Not yet? Cali's gaze found his. "But you'd like to?"

"Sure. Some day. How about you?" He stepped close, studying her with an intensity she felt down to her toes.

"At least three, maybe four."

He laughed. "You are a brave one, Cali Stevens. My kind of girl."

Her face heated. "I don't think I'm that brave." *But I wouldn't mind being your kind of girl.* She looked away before her face heated even further.

She glanced at the other pictures and her heart skipped. One of the frames had a picture of Nick with his arm around a beautiful brunette.

"Who's this?" she asked in the smoothest voice she could muster.

"My ex-girlfriend. I need to take the picture out of the frame. It's a hassle to get it out, and I haven't done it yet."

"How long ago did you break up?"

"A little over a year."

"Were you close?"

He shrugged. "Not overly so. We dated for a while, but..."

"What happened?"

"At first I enjoyed being with her. I felt comfortable around her, and we shared many common interests. But, the more I got to know her, the more I realized what we valued in life was different."

Cali straightened, turning her gaze from the picture. "Different how?"

"I want to live life God's way. She doesn't." Nick's gaze locked onto hers.

"How long did it take you to realize it?"

"Not as long as it took me to tell her. I didn't want to hurt her, but I shouldn't have let it continue as long as it did. She wanted me to meet all of her needs, and she didn't understand why I couldn't."

"What kind of needs?"

"Emotional mostly. She expected me to be some sort of a hero. Someone larger than life. I tried to explain only God can meet all of our needs."

"I remember hearing in church God created us with a void only He can fill."

"That's right, and she didn't understand that."

"What about all of the other women?"

His mouth quirked into a grin and he looked her over. "*All* of the other women?"

"The ones Mrs. Mayes tossed at you?"

He chuckled. "Why? Are you jealous?"

Cali turned away, shrugging. "Why would I be jealous?" she asked, silently wondering about her own motives.

Nick placed his hands on her shoulders and turned her to face him. "Well, to answer your first question, I turned them away because I'm not interested in casual relationships. I'd rather find a woman who shares my faith to build a life with. Second question..." He released her and rubbed his hand across his jaw. "Let's see. Why would you be jealous?"

Cali's cell phone rang and made her jump. She pulled it from her back pocket and checked the caller ID. She didn't recognize the number, but wanted a way out of answering Nick's question so she answered it.

"Have you reconsidered my offer?" The man's voice sounded somewhat familiar.

"Who is this?"

"Lex Harrison. But you can call me Lex."

Irritation coursed through her. "How did you get this number?"

Nick stepped closer, concern clouding his playful mood.

"I'm a reporter remember? I have my resources."

"I gave you my answer. It won't change," she snapped.

Lex let out a loud sigh. "That's too bad. I thought maybe since you and the sheriff are getting along so well..."

Cali closed the phone.

Nick's gaze shifted from the phone back to her. "Who was that?"

"Lex Harrison. A nosy reporter."

"For the newspaper. I've heard of him. He has a reputation as being very aggressive. What did he want?"

Cali stuffed her phone back into her pocket. "He wants inside information."

He crossed his arms over his chest and shook his head. "Don't they all?"

Taken aback, Cali answered, "I'm a reporter and that's not what I'm after. I just want Serena to be safe."

Nick's features softened. "I didn't mean you, Cali. When I think about you, your career as a reporter is the last thing that crosses my mind," he said in a low voice.

Warmth spread through her, and she relaxed again, until she caught a whiff of smoke. "Is something burning?"

His face fell. "The bread!" He ran over to the oven, just in time to keep it from broiling to death. "I hope you like your toast a deep, golden brown."

Thankful for the distraction from Lex Harrison's call, Cali followed Nick into the kitchen and leaned over the pan. "They look fine." The melted butter and garlic aroma made her mouth water.

"Let's eat." Nick turned, setting the pan on the stove. He walked to the table and offered Cali a seat.

"Thank you." She slipped into the chair and waited as he carried the food to the table, then sat across from her.

He clasped his hands and bowed his head. Cali forced her thoughts away from the phone call, and followed Nick's lead. He asked God to bless the food, thanked Him and handed a bowl of noodles to her. "Ladies first."

"Thanks."

After they had eaten in comfortable silence for a few minutes, he glanced toward the door. "The storm's been upgraded to a low category hurricane. The mayor has issued a voluntary evacuation."

Cali swallowed a bite of crusty bread as a panic tore through her. "I won't leave Serena."

He sighed. "I know you won't. But," his expression grew serious, "if the hurricane heads directly for us, my hands will be tied trying to get people off the island. So will all of my deputies. Then the aftermath..." he trailed off.

"What are you saying?"

"I'm saying the hurricane could delay our search for Serena."

Shocked by the thought, Cali set down her fork. "I hadn't considered that. I've been so caught up in trying to find her, I didn't think about how the storm could interfere. There's been so much else to worry about." She dabbed her mouth with a napkin and turned, looking outside.

Nick took her hand, the warm, gentle pressure giving her much needed reassurance. She swept her gaze to his and warmth spread from her hands through her entire body.

"You look so afraid. Let everything else go, and think about one question." He leaned closer. "You're willing to trust me. But, are you willing to trust God?"

His question surprised her. "No matter what you say, I can't just sit back and wait." She tore from his grasp and stood. "I'm stronger than you think."

"I know you're strong. Trusting God doesn't make you weak, Cali. It makes you stronger. He gives you an inner strength, a confidence you can't get anywhere else."

She turned and walked across the room, looking out the glass door to the rough ocean water. Dusk settled in, and the ocean grew darker with each passing moment as Cali watched and considered what Nick had said. Drawing in a breath, she admitted, "I want to trust Him. I just have issues giving up control."

Nick moved behind her, wrapping his arms around her and pulling her back against his chest. "Don't think you're the only one with control issues. I battle with it every day."

"You do?"

"Sure."

"I thought you learned your lesson in the bar fight that gave you your scar."

"I learned I have limitations, but it's still hard to accept them."

"But, you seem to have so much faith." She rested her head against his shoulder.

"I do have faith. But that doesn't mean I'm perfect."

"No one's perfect."

"That's right. So, we do what we can and pray God helps us along the way."

"Are you referring to finding Serena?"

"I'm referring to life."

They fell into silence as Nick continued to hold Cali in his arms. His warmth surrounded her, coaxing her to relax. His breath touched her skin as he whispered, "Consider this fair warning."

"Fair warning?" She turned in his arms.

He dropped his head and pressed his lips to hers, drawing his hand behind her neck to bring her close.

Nick had promised he would warn her before kissing her again. Pleasure and guilt tore into Cali at the same time. He had taken her by surprise with his kiss earlier. But, now that she had been warned, shouldn't she stop him? Should she be enjoying his affections when Serena was still missing? Tears burned her eyes and she backed away, gathering her breath. "I can't help but feel guilty."

"Don't." He inched back. Cali expected to see irritation in his features, yet only compassion came through. "My men are out there searching, hunting. When it's my turn, I'll be back out there. Not a minute goes by when someone isn't looking for her."

"You'll be back out there. What about me? I feel so...restricted."

He sighed and stepped away. "This control issue you have will tear you apart if you let it." He began gathering the dishes and putting away the food.

Confused by her own reactions, Cali turned from the door and paced the room. A part of her wanted to walk straight back into Nick's arms, but her conscience wouldn't let her.

A computer desk sat in the far corner, and a pile of pictures lay scattered across it. She walked to it, and recognized that the pictures had been taken at the press conference. Before thumbing through them, she stopped and asked, "Nick?"

"Yeah. Go ahead and look at them. If it will make you feel better." The dishes clanked and clattered as he loaded them into the dishwasher, making Cali wonder if he was a bit irritated with her after all.

Regardless, she kept her focus on the pictures and sank into his plush desk chair. She leaned forward and picked them up. Her hands shook as she looked from one to another, scanning the faces in each picture. She stopped when she recognized three of the people in the background. Trey, Chad, and Anna stood together behind the throng of reporters. She struggled to remain calm and rational. *Think, Cali. What possible reason could the lifeguards have to be at the press conference?*

Cali stood and carried the picture with her to the kitchen. She waited for Nick to finish loading the dishwasher and add the detergent. After he set the washer on the normal cycle, she said, "I met these lifeguards. The one on the left is Trey, Anna's in the middle, and the one on the right is Chad."

If Nick was surprised she had met them and knew their names, he didn't show it. "I know who they are. It's another dead end, Cali. Let it go."

"I won't let it go. How do you know it's a dead end?"

He ran a hand down his face. "Because I've already checked into it like I have everything else. Let's get some fresh air." He turned, walked across the living room and slid the door open, stepping outside.

She set the picture on the counter and followed.

The sounds of the ocean met her in full force as the wind tossed her hair into her face, and she struggled to keep it from her eyes. Darkness had fallen, and the water appeared black and fathomless, except for the white, cresting waves gleaming in the night.

Nick leaned on the railing. "Each lifeguard is assigned a rotating shift," he explained. "I obtained the schedule for the past three months from their headquarters. They have dozens of lifeguards working different shifts and times. None of the lifeguard's work schedules matched up with the dates, places and times each of the women had been abducted."

"But that doesn't mean…"

"And each of the guys in the pictures, Chad Livingston and Trey Bradley, had alibis for the time frame the women were abducted."

"Alibis can be faked."

"I know." He sighed, running a hand through his hair. "But we have to move on to other more likely suspects if we're going to catch this guy."

"Have you brought anyone in for questioning?"

"Not yet. We haven't had enough probable cause."

Cali gripped the railing next to him. "You seem to always be one step ahead of me."

His smile showed his agreement, but he said nothing.

She turned to the pounding surf again. "Regardless of what you think, Nick. I do believe in you, and in your abilities."

"If you mean that, then do me a favor."

"OK."

"Leave the investigation to me, and try to keep yourself out of trouble."

"I'm not looking for trouble, Nick. I'm only looking for answers."

"Sometimes we don't have the answers to our questions, no matter how bad we want them, or how long we search for them. Sometimes we have to find peace even without knowing what is happening to someone, or has happened to someone. We have to find peace without understanding why."

"How Nick? I'm so scared for Serena..."

"By putting our trust in God. Cali, even if things don't turn out the way we want them to, we have to trust that God has a reason for everything he lets happen. Even if we don't understand why."

"I want to trust Him Nick. I just don't know how..."

"Then pray that He helps you learn to trust Him. He loves you, Cali."

Nick's cell phone rang and he stepped away to answer the call before Cali had a chance to reply. She watched him through a haze of confusion. Deep down, she knew he was right. She needed to put her trust in God. She had learned to trust Nick in the few days she had known him. So, why was it so hard to trust her Creator?

Cali's thoughts kept her attention until Nick's back stiffened and he stilled. A heartbeat later, he turned to face her as he listened to the caller. Fear tore through her at the dire expression spreading across his face. Cali's breath caught deep in her lungs as she waited for an explanation.

Chapter Eighteen

"I'll be right in." Cali barely made out the gruff words spoken above the waves crashing against the shoreline. Nick closed his cell phone and pocketed it. He turned and rested his hands against the porch railing, leaning into it as he blew out a deep breath. He kept his eyes trained on the churning ocean.

Cali stepped around him, catching sight of his profile as a strike of lightning exposed his now pale features. With his vibrant color drained away, he looked bone-tired and weary. She touched his shoulder as trepidation tightened her chest, making it difficult to breathe.

Had they found Serena? Was she alive? She wanted to ask. She wanted to shake out the answers. But, an immobilizing fear froze all possible movements. The fear clawed its way to the surface of her heart, scratching and tearing at her emotions. A sob formed in her throat, and remained suspended for a fraction of a second before escaping her lips.

At the sound, Nick turned and took her face in his hands. Warm, strong hands that had a slight shake in them, causing a terrifying fear bolting to her core. If this experienced man, full of strength and confidence trembled, what kind of news must he have heard?

Paralyzed, she waited.

He ran his thumbs along her tear-streaked face as his eyes locked with hers. "Another woman has been reported missing." His voice was gravelly, and held traces of remorse and guilt.

A torrent of emotions stormed within her, leaving her feeling as if caught in the middle of a crashing wave, tumbling out of control. "Another woman?"

"Yes. Deputy Owen said she fits the profile of the offender's previous victims. Alone. Unsuspecting. Defenseless." A spark of anger flashed in his eyes.

"Then the call wasn't about Serena?"

"No. There's no more information about her location. But…" his words trailed off and he pulled away. Tucking his hands into his pockets, he raised his voice, combating the rising wind and surf as the storm grew closer. "Cali, there is something else you should know."

Her breath caught. "W-what?" The question tumbled from her mouth even though she wasn't sure she wanted to know the answer.

"By abducting this woman before releasing Serena, he's altered his pattern."

"What does that mean?"

His voice grew in intensity. "Any change in the offender's routine could mean we're closing in on him. He may be getting desperate. Or, his behavior may change for other reasons. Each time he successfully commits a crime, he becomes more confident, more self-assured. This makes him extremely dangerous and unpredictable. Each new risk he takes indicates that his twisted need for power and control is deepening."

Cali's fear heightened close to hysteria. Her gaze darted across his features, looking for something solid to focus on in such an unstable environment. Her gaze landed on his, and she recognized the confidence she had been searching for. Drawing strength from him, she found her voice, "What are you going to do?"

"Find them."

The wind kicked up, and the rain came, dropping in solid sheets from the dark clouds above, making it impossible to remain outside. Nick put his arm around her waist and led her back to the sliding door. He slipped it open and ushered her inside.

The sudden, quiet stillness should have helped calm her, but her new fears for Serena's safety made her heart continue to beat at an erratic pace. She wiped raindrops from her face as the wind drove the rain against the glass door in a whipped frenzy.

"I have to go." Concern etched across his features.

She wanted to go too, but didn't ask. He needed to focus on his job without worrying about her. She ran a hand across his chest, pretending to smooth out a wrinkle on his T-shirt. "Be safe."

Nick covered her hand with his, securing her palm against him. "You'll be all right?"

She nodded, drawing strength from the steady heartbeat beneath her fingers.

"Wait for the rain to let up before you go back upstairs. Flip the lock on my door on your way out. When you get upstairs, lock your door, double-check the windows, and call me if anything happens. Call me if you even think something *may* happen." He stepped closer, pressing his warm lips to hers.

Cali lifted her hand to his rough, unshaven cheek, inched back and whispered, "Will you come back to me tonight? No matter how late?"

"I'll come," he promised. He pulled on his socks and shoes, grabbed his keys and gave her a long, lingering look before slipping back into the throes of the storm.

****

Something woke her. Darkness engulfed her with a stillness that could only mean the band of rain had passed. Cali heard the faint sound of the ocean and the slow, steady dripping of lingering water droplets hitting the porch. The illuminated clock glowed in the darkened room. The bright green lights showed the time. Four o'clock a.m.

Nick.

Cali had grown accustomed to his presence, and her instincts told her he had not returned yet. She sat upright, trying not to make a sound as she listened for what may have wakened her. A faint noise came from outside the sliding glass door. She held her breath, waiting. Then a tall, dark shadow appeared in front of the door, and a light tap sounded on the glass.

Fear pounded through her until her mind caught up with her wakening body. Would an intruder bother to knock?

"Cali, it's me."

She recognized Nick's voice immediately, as if she had been hearing it all of her life. Releasing the breath she had been holding, she stood so fast she felt lightheaded. Bending over, she stumbled to the door and unlocked it.

"What's wrong?" he asked with concern. He wrapped an arm across her back and leaned with her.

"Nothing. I waited for you on the sofa. I must've fallen asleep and just stood up too fast." She lifted upright and studied him through the slice of moonlight filtering through the doorway.

The dark circles under Nick's eyes indicated his fatigue. A sense of defeat surrounded him.

"You didn't find them."

He shook his head. "We followed all the leads we could." He raked a hand through his hair and shrugged. "It's almost as if he's a ghost."

"He's not a ghost. He's real, and he's got Serena and," she paused, "and what's the other woman's name? Who is she?"

"She's a tourist from out-of-state. Her name's

Marlene Stanton. Thirty-eight years old. She came here for a weekend getaway. Alone." He shook his head. "Why did she come alone? Didn't I make it clear at the press conference how dangerous it is for a woman to be here alone? And the headlines in the papers...how could she have not known?"

Cali stepped closer. "Nick. A lot of people don't watch the news or read the paper when they go on vacation."

"I should have prevented this. I should have..."

"It is not your fault this woman was abducted. It's not your fault any of them were taken."

"That's not what you said about Serena's abduction before."

"I'm sorry. I never should have said you could've prevented it. I never should've implied it was your fault. I didn't mean it. I meant to apologize before now, but it never seemed to be the right time."

He continued as if she hadn't spoken. "If only I could have..."

"What? What could you have done? You've done everything you can do." She gave a brief, humorless laugh. "You're the one telling me neither of us is in control. You're the one telling me I'm carrying around too much responsibility on my shoulders. What about you?"

He shook his head. "This is different. I'm the sheriff, Cali. It's my job."

"Yes. But you have limitations, too." She ran her fingers under his shirtsleeve, touching the scar from his old wound. "Remember?"

He jerked back. "I'll always remember." Anger lined his features, and he clenched his hands into white-knuckled fists. He turned and paced across the room, stopping short of the kitchen.

Cali sunk into the middle of the sofa, amd clutching her head between her hands, she prayed, *Lord, help me know what to do for him. Help me to know what to say.*

A few moments later, Nick sat next to her. His firm thigh came to rest against hers. She looked up as he leaned his elbows on his knees and turned to face her.

"I'm sorry. I shouldn't have brought up your past," she said.

"No. It's OK. I appreciate the reminder. It helps keep me in line."

"In line with what?"

"In line with God's will." He reached an arm around her and pulled her back to rest with him on the couch.

She tucked her right shoulder under his arm and rested her cheek against his chest.

"Cali?"

"Mmm?" She looked up into his face at the same time he looked down into hers. His gaze roamed over her features as if he were memorizing each curve, each line. He lifted a hand to brush an errant strand of hair from her cheek. His fingers slid over her skin, leaving a trail of heat in their wake. Cali parted her lips in anticipation when his gaze landed on them. She closed her eyes. His heated breath touched her skin. Then he pressed his lips to hers.

Warm. Caressing. But different from when he had kissed her before. He didn't hesitate, but she noted a slight vulnerability coming through. When he pulled away, Cali opened her eyes, and detected the same vulnerability in his gaze that she had discovered in his touch.

"Will you pray with me?" His whispered words broke through the quiet stillness.

Cali straightened, stirred by the uncertainty coming through his voice. "Of course."

She watched as he threaded the fingers of his right hand with the fingers of her left. His thumb caressed her skin in slow circles as he whispered, "Lord, please grant us the serenity to accept the things we cannot change, the courage to change the things we can..."

"And the wisdom to know the difference." Cali followed the rest of the prayer with him in tandem.

They sat in silence for several long minutes. Cali thought of the significance of the prayer. She had heard the Serenity Prayer many times throughout her life, but had never realized the true meaning of the words.

As much as she hated to admit it, she couldn't control the outcome of every situation. Nick couldn't either. They both needed God to guide them in understanding the difference between the things they could control and the things they couldn't.

Cali sensed the tension in Nick's body ease, and she remained still in his arms until she heard his steady, even breathing. She looked at his closed eyes, and saw that he slept with the peacefulness of a man who fully trusted in the Lord.

Nick's simple, honest request to pray with him had affected her more deeply than any other words he could have spoken, and she felt herself falling for the hard, well-organized and no-nonsense Sheriff of Coral Isle.

Chapter Nineteen

Nick woke as the sun peeked over the horizon. Rays of light danced across the room, shining on Cali's sleeping form. He blinked, both to clear his eyes and to reassure himself that what he experienced last night was real. Had he really found a caring, compassionate woman, content to simply settle into his arms and pray? Had he found someone to lift him up when discouragement threatened to overcome him?

An intense satisfaction washed over him as he remembered her willingness and sincerity in praying with him. With her encouragement, he had found renewed strength to continue the hunt for the kidnapper.

Remaining as still as possible, Nick savored the warmth of Cali in his arms and the soft look of contentment on her relaxed features. He wanted to linger, to simply enjoy the feel of her in his arms. But, the room darkened as a cloud eased past the sun, reminding him of the growing threat of the approaching storm. The wind had strengthened—not to an alarming level—but, nevertheless, danger lurked in the distance. His senses went on alert, and his muscles tensed.

He wiped the sleep from his eyes and tried to remain objective. Falling asleep with Cali last night had not been the smartest thing to do, even though it had felt right.

Feelings can get you in trouble, Nick.

He remembered the phrase his father had instilled in him as a child. He had heard it so often that it had become ingrained in him. He needed to keep his feelings for Cali in perspective. If he allowed himself to get too involved, he would have a heavy dose of heartache when she left to return to Brookstone.

He slid his arm out from under Cali, trying to steel himself against the intoxicating effect she had on him. He walked to the glass door, watching the dark clouds form a thick barrier to the sun. He needed to focus on the dangers from the approaching storm and from the kidnapper. He had to find the missing women. He prayed for courage and wisdom again as he slipped quietly out the door, locking it as he left.

Nick walked down the steps to the first floor, going directly to the kitchen. He listened with half an ear to his voice messages as he started a pot of coffee.

"Nick. We have a leak." Helen's cautious words played over the digital machine.

"A leak?" Confusion threatened his weary mind. "A leak in the roof?" he asked his empty kitchen. Nick shook his head trying to clear it. "I need more sleep." He grabbed the glass carafe from the coffee maker and filled his mug. He breathed in the heady aroma, trying to inhale energy.

The message continued, "You need to take a look at this morning's paper." Helen had hung up without saying goodbye.

The black coffee burned his throat as he took a deep, hasty gulp before setting the mug on the kitchen counter. Nick stepped outside and took the stairs two at a time, then crossed the driveway to his newspaper. He pulled the paper from the plastic sleeve and unfolded it.

He read the headlines. His mind reeled. His jaw clenched. His trust had been betrayed.

****

Cali jumped and nearly fell off the sofa when a brisk knock sounded at the door. She twisted around. Nick's broad form stood outside. He knocked again, his fist banging against the door.

"I'm coming." She rubbed her eyes, and yawned as she stood. Her bare feet padded on the cool, tiled floor as she crossed the room. Nick's features became distinguishable beyond the dew-covered glass as she came close. Her smile faded.

Something had happened since last night. The tenderness she had witnessed in Nick had vanished. Lines creased his brow, and he held his square jaw clenched. He slapped a rolled up newspaper against his palm as he waited.

Her pulse increased and time slowed as she reached for the door. She flipped the lock, and Nick pulled the door wide before she had a chance to. The strong wind blew sand into the entranceway, dusting her feet with its gritty texture, and the once lifeless, gray clouds in the sky had darkened into a threatening hue.

Nick stepped forward. She stepped back.

His presence filled the room, demanding her attention. His anger radiated through her, all the way to her bare toes.

"I thought we understood each other. I thought I understood you." His low, intimidating voice confused her.

"What do you mean?" she asked, not understanding the reason for his change in disposition.

"The paper, Cali. Don't tell me you're surprised at the headlines." His mouth formed a tight, thin line as he unfolded the paper and tapped his index finger on the big black lettering.

"High Tide Stalker Strikes Again," Cali read the words aloud, and then met his intense gaze. "Another woman?"

He shook his head and read part of the article. "Marlene Stanton is the fourth woman to be abducted by a man who has released each of his first two victims...at...high...tide," he pronounced the last three words slowly, as if he intended her to hear them clearly.

"But we already knew about Marlene..."

"High tide, Cali. You're the only one outside of my office who knew that specific detail," he cut her off with his rising voice.

Her gaze darted to the article and back, as if she could decipher a deeper meaning from the black print on the paper. "You believe I leaked the information?"

"We've never had this happen before."

"So you think it was me?" she asked again, looking for absolute clarification.

"I trust my staff, Cali."

She heard Nick's words. She also heard what he didn't say. He didn't trust her. Pain ripped through her, as if he had gouged a hole in her heart. She shook her head as hot tears burned her eyes. "How can you think...?"

"I follow the evidence remember?"

"Nick. I didn't..."

"I believed I could trust you." He flipped the paper to a nearby table and crossed his arms.

"You can trust me, Nick. I didn't tell..." she picked up the paper and read the reporter's name, "Lex Harrison...?" Her heart plummeted and her words trailed off as images of big, shiny teeth and a bulbous nose came rushing back. The reporter had discovered inside information after all. But how?

Nick remained guarded, looking her over as if searching for a way to prove the truth.

Cali softened her voice. "I thought we had

something between us. Something special."

His lips tightened. "Don't change the subject."

Cali's injured pride turned into a simmering anger. "I guess I was wrong."

"This has nothing to do with what's happening between us."

"It has everything to do with it. If you had fallen for me like I have for you, you wouldn't doubt me."

Nick's silence filled the room, broken only by the wind from the open door rattling the newspaper in Cali's hand.

"That's right. I'll admit it." A fresh wave of tears filled her eyes, and she swiped them away. She held her breath, waiting for reassurances.

"I can't do this now, Cali," his whispered words crushed her more than his accusations had. "I have to catch the stalker. I need to focus." He ran a hand through his hair. "And I can't when I'm worrying about you."

"You mean, when you're worrying about who I'm leaking information to?" She lifted her chin and crossed her arms in defense.

"You spoke with Lex Harrison yesterday."

"Yes. But I didn't tell him anything. I need you to believe me."

"This is getting way too complicated." He shook his head and stared out toward the ocean.

"What is? You and me? Or the case?"

His gaze snapped back. "I can't allow distractions to keep me from doing my job."

"I never meant to keep you from your job. I never meant to be a distraction." *I never meant to fall in love with you.* She retreated a few steps, trying to distance herself from him, and from the ache building in her heart.

When Nick studied her in silence, Cali decided to try one more time to convince him. "What motivation would I have for telling Lex Harrison anything, anyway?"

He blew out a deep breath, and ran a hand through his hair. "I don't know. All I know is you had recent contact with him, and you're the only outsider who knew about the releases at high tide."

His words shook her to her core. "Outsider?" Her anger deflated, leaving her hollow and spent. Her legs weakened, and she sank onto the sofa. "Just find Serena, and you won't have to deal with me anymore."

"Cali I..." He hesitated. "We'll talk later. I have to get to work. Deputy Owen will come by to check on you."

Her mouth went dry. "That's not necessary."

"I'd feel better if he does."

"Well, as long as *you* feel better."

"He's no threat to you. If I thought he was, I wouldn't let him near you."

"That's comforting."

"What do you have against him, anyway?"

"Nothing. Just go." She stood and walked to the bedroom, hoping that slamming the door would make her feel better.

It didn't.

Chapter Twenty

"Coffee?" Helen asked from the doorway of Nick's office.

He glanced up from an accident report he was filling out. The approaching storm had already begun causing damage, and calls were picking up. "Thanks."

Helen stepped in and set the cup on his desk, then settled into the wooden chair across from him. "I see from the scowl on your face that you read the newspaper's headlines."

Nick picked up the mug full of fresh coffee and sat back in his chair. The rich aroma enticed him, and he took a sip. The steaming liquid warmed his throat, but did nothing to improve his mood. "It's my fault."

"Now, why do you say that?" Helen lifted her eyebrows.

"I let her get to me. I told her about the stalker releasing his victims at high tide."

"By her, I assume you mean Ms. Stevens?"

He took another sip before setting the mug down. He crossed his arms over his chest and leaned back. "I knew better."

"Why on earth do you think it was her?" Helen tapped her fingers on the armrests and tilted her head.

"Who else?"

"Did you read the entire article?"

"Not yet, but..."

Helen sprang from the chair and shuffled away before he had a chance to finish his sentence. A moment later, she returned, carrying the morning's paper. The headlines speared him again, and he held back any visible reaction to it. A difficult task, considering betrayal slammed into him each time he read the black and white proof of the leaked information.

"Read it." Helen slapped the newspaper on his desk.

Nick leaned forward. He would not tolerate someone making demands of him in his own office, unless that someone was Helen. She had earned his respect through the years of working together, and that alone bought her ample leeway.

He scanned the article, jumping over the basic filler information. Reading a few details about the press conference, he noticed a few quotes from Deputy Owen. His heart lurched, and anger seeped through him. "Deputy Owen told the reporter Cali is staying with me," he said the words slowly.

Alarm heightened his awareness. He didn't want anyone knowing where Cali was staying. At this point, he considered every man on the island a threat, and now the information had gone public.

Helen stood over his desk, leaned in and poked a rounded finger at each of the three places Deputy Owen's name appeared. "Maybe you'd better redirect your accusations, Sheriff."

He looked into Helen's sturdy gaze. "He's been with the department for over two years. Why would he reveal the information?"

"He gave up Cali's location, didn't he? The way he eats up the spotlight, he'd be my first guess as the one who leaked the high tide details."

The possibility of Cali's innocence gave Nick an

enormous measure of relief. "Send him in. I want a word with him."

Helen headed for the door, but turned before she reached it. "I hope you didn't go accusing Ms. Stevens right away, without thinking about the consequences first."

His stomach fell. "I did."

"I was afraid of that, judging from the look on your face when you dragged yourself in the door this morning." She scratched the side of her head, her manicured fingernails displacing a few strands of graying hair. "At least there are perks that come along with apologies." She gave an exaggerated wink and grinned.

He brushed her playfulness aside. "Cali's a distraction. I need to focus."

"Cali's not the reason you haven't caught the stalker yet, Sheriff." She turned and left the office.

He considered her words until Deputy Owen sauntered into the room and turned Nick's focus back to his present circumstances.

"You needed to see me, Sheriff?"

"Have a seat."

Deputy Owen glanced around the office, his gaze landing on the newspaper. Then, he looked everywhere except at Nick.

"I'll give you one chance to tell me the truth."

Attention captured, Owen turned his long, narrow face toward him. "It slipped."

Nick straightened and leaned forward in his chair. Clasping his hands in front of him he said, "Care to elaborate?"

"Look, the guy approached me, OK?"

"Of course he did. He's a reporter," Nick ground out the words. "Why would you tell him where Cali is staying? You knew she was already in danger."

"That kind of slipped too."

Nick rose from his chair.

Owen flinched.

It took every ounce of restraint Nick had not to lean over the desk and throttle the man. "Let me make this clear. You will never leak information to the press again. Understood?"

Owen swallowed, his Adam's apple bouncing in his throat. "Yes, sir."

"You will face disciplinary action after the storm has passed." Nick needed every man on duty with the hurricane approaching. He walked around his desk and stood, towering over him. "You'd better watch your step, Owen."

Nick stalked from his office, anger radiating around him. "I'm heading out, Helen. You know how to reach me."

He used the time in his truck to pray for guidance. He had hurt Cali by accusing her of leaking the information, and had not listened when she denied it. Guilt overwhelmed him, anger burned him, and tension threatened another raging headache.

Nick gripped the wheel with tense hands, as angry with himself as he was with Owen. He should have listened to Cali. He should have suspected Owen. After all, Cali had no reason to leak the information, and Owen had always reveled in being the center of attention.

Nick hoped Cali would forgive him. He had damaged their newfound relationship, and he prayed she would understand and be forgiving, which would be the only way to mend the gap he had gouged between them. He pulled into the driveway, and his anxiety in confronting her disintegrated.

Cali's car was gone.

Nick's cell phone rang. Irritated by the setback, he snapped, "Sheriff Justice."

"Mayor Wilson has issued a mandatory evacuation of Coral Isle," Helen's strained voice came over the line. "The hurricane's heading directly for us."

He blew out a deep breath. "I expected the order. Get the deputies out there, Helen. I want to provide as much assistance as possible to those willing to leave."

"And for those unwilling?"

"The shelters will be open. Let's pray the people will go."

"I can do that," Helen said.

"I'll get things prepared at my cottage since I'm already here. Then head back out."

"Stay safe out there, Sheriff." Helen voiced her concern.

"I will." He pressed the end button, and then dialed Cali's number.

The phone rang but no one answered. The voicemail picked up. "Cali, it's Nick. I need to talk to you. Call me as soon as you can." After he hung up, he thought about the way he had left her that morning. Hurt and alone. Angry. Anxious to talk to her again and to apologize, he hoped she would return his call soon.

Nick stepped out of his truck and climbed up the steps to his cottage to prepare for the potentially damaging winds. He gathered the potted flowers that lined his porch, as well as the other small items that might be tossed around by the wind, and stored them inside. He always locked his windows and doors, but double-checked them anyway. He stepped outside and cranked the hurricane shutters over the sliding glass door and windows, hoping the aluminum slats would keep the glass from shattering as the hurricane produced flying debris.

Finished, Nick faced the churning ocean, watching wave after wave pound the shoreline. The dune stretching across the front of his cottage had been reinforced last year with additional sand, but he prayed it would be enough to hold back the rising tide.

He climbed the steps to Cali's level and made

sure the windows were also shut and locked. He cranked the shutters over the windows facing the ocean, but left the sliding glass door uncovered, leaving a way for Cali to get inside when she returned.

A sudden fear struck him.

What if she had left? He didn't believe she would, but she had been so upset this morning...

Nick slipped inside and checked the bedroom for her belongings. Relief washed through him. Cali hadn't packed her bags. She would be back. He shook his head at his own range of emotions. Hadn't he wanted her to leave just a few short days ago? Now he was standing in his cottage, praying she hadn't left.

Nick pulled his cell phone from his pocket, in case he hadn't heard her call above the roaring ocean and wind. No messages. No missed calls.

The sliding glass door scraped open. He spun on his heel. "Cali?"

"Searching for evidence?" She appeared in the bedroom doorway.

He stepped toward her. She flinched. He stopped and held up his hands. "I came home and you weren't here. I tried calling, but you didn't answer. I thought you might have left."

"Sorry to disappoint you." She revealed no traces of the anger she'd had that morning; only cool detachment remained.

Guilt poked him. He would have rather seen anger in her eyes than the distance they portrayed. "I'm not disappointed. I'm glad you're still here."

"You are?"

This time Nick stepped toward her and didn't stop until he came near. "I know you didn't leak the High Tide Stalker information." He wanted to reach out. He wanted to touch her, but kept his hands at his sides.

She glanced around him at her belongings.

"You're not looking for evidence?"

"No, I'm not. Deputy Owen admitted to the slip."

Her brows lifted. "Owen?" Her gaze showed temporary interest, and then clouded over with pain. She hugged her arms. "Trust is a fragile thing, isn't it?"

"It is. But it can be restored. With time...and forgiveness." He paused. "I'm sorry, Cali," he whispered.

She studied him for a moment as if deciding his level of sincerity then dropped her gaze and turned. She walked to the dimly lit living room, and he followed. "I see you're preparing for the hurricane."

"The weather forecasters are calling for it to hit tonight. The mayor has called a mandatory evacuation."

"Don't ask me to leave." She turned to face him with renewed spirit.

"I won't. But I want you to go to the station. It's safer there."

"Where will you be?"

"I'll go there too, but only after the bridge closes. I want to get as many people as possible to safety."

Her eyes widened. "What about Mrs. Mayes?"

"I need to check on her," Nick answered, touched by her concern for the woman she had only met once. "She won't drive in this weather."

"How will she get off the island?"

"She probably won't."

"But, she lives on the water. Her cottage might flood. It's not safe for her to stay there. Will shelters be open?"

He grimaced. "Yeah. But trying to convince her to go to one is difficult. A few years ago, we had an evacuation for a hurricane, and she refused to leave her home. I ended up staying with her overnight, just to make sure she was all right."

"I'll take her." Cali grabbed her purse. "Give me directions to her place, and to the nearest shelter. If she refuses, I'll pack her bags for her and bring her to the station with me."

"You don't have to do this."

"I know. But I want to. Aren't you worried about her?"

"Yeah, I am. But I'm worried about you, too. Cali, I'm sorry for accusing you."

She placed a hand on his forearm. "I know. We'll work it out later, OK?"

Nick liked the fact she used the word 'we.' Encouraged, he placed a slow, soft kiss on her lips. She didn't lean into him as he had hoped, but she didn't push him away either.

"I'll give you directions to Mrs. Mayes's cottage, but I want you back before it gets dark." Nick took her arms in his grasp and looked straight into her eyes. "Promise me."

"I promise."

He wanted to say more. He wanted to melt the cool reserve in her gaze. But, it would have to wait. He quickly wrote the directions on a notepad and handed it to her. "Get going. I'll see you at the station later."

Nick stepped outside with Cali, and locked the door behind them. He cranked the shutter closed over the sliding door as Cali disappeared out of sight. He took a final look around his property before leaving. The wind blew scraps of wood and debris across his land, and he prayed his home would survive the storm.

The clouds no longer merely threatened rain as they relented to the tremendous pressure and expelled the moisture that had been gathering. He ducked his head against the rain and headed downstairs, preparing for the long day ahead.

Chapter Twenty-One

Cali found Mrs. Mayes's cottage without getting lost, which amazed her, considering she had driven on ten different roads to get here. Prepared to convince Mrs. Mayes to seek shelter, Cali pulled into the drive.

She stepped out, and a wind gust blew sand into her eyes. She squinted, trying to see past the gritty, painful specks. She rushed to the porch and pounded on the door, waited a moment, and then knocked again.

Mrs. Mayes didn't answer.

Cali stepped around to the back of the cottage, and her cell phone rang. "Hello?" She rubbed her achy eyes, trying to clear them.

"Hey. It's me," Nick's voice sent a wave of warmth through her. She was struggling to hold onto her anger after his heartfelt apology earlier, but found it difficult as she heard the welcoming sound of his voice.

"Hey. Mrs. Mayes isn't answering her door."

"She just called. Her oldest son has already taken her off the island. Sorry I didn't know before. I could've saved you a trip."

Relieved Mrs. Mayes was safe, Cali blew out a breath. "It's all right. I'm just glad she's somewhere safe, and with someone who loves her."

"That's where I want you to be," his voice softened close to a whisper.

"Where? Somewhere safe or with someone who loves me?" Her heartbeat intensified as she waited for an answer.

"Both. Come on in to the station Cali. I'll be out on calls for most of the afternoon, but I'll be there later."

The warmth that had spread through her when she had first heard his voice returned in full force. "I'll see you later then."

"Drive safe," he said, and then hung up.

Nick's implied words echoed through Cali's head, and she could not focus on the drive back across the island. He wanted her to be with someone who loved her. He wanted her to be with him. Did that mean that he loved her? The realization struck, leaving her reeling and lightheaded. She had arrived on the island looking for Serena, and had found love along the way. Or, had she? Only this morning, Nick had accused her of leaking information to the press. Yes, he had apologized for jumping to conclusions, but he obviously didn't put much trust in her.

Cali bit her lower lip. Balancing her countless emotions had taken a toll on her. She was terrified she would never see Serena again, and afraid she would allow her feelings for Nick to interfere with her search. But, she loved him, and wanted him to love her back. She blew out a breath, trying to sort out her swirling emotions. *Lord, please help. Please bring Serena back. Please let Nick love me.*

As her thoughts scattered, so did her sense of direction. Cali was lost before she realized she had taken a wrong turn. She pulled into a gas station to study the directions Nick had given her. It didn't help. She would have asked a gas station employee for directions, but the boarded windows and doors indicated the station was closed.

Picking up her cell phone, she dialed her dad's

number, needing direction in more ways than one.

"Stevens here."

"Dad? It's good to hear your voice." Cali let the engine idle as she closed her eyes.

"Hey, hon'. Are you safe from the hurricane? Your mother's threatening to come after you."

"Tell her I'm fine. I have a safe place to stay."

"What's the update on Serena?"

She sighed as tears threatened. "Nothing new."

"Are you sure you're OK? Is the sheriff treating you right?"

"He's looking after me," she said with honesty, avoiding the earlier incident.

"Good to hear."

Cali slowly opened her eyes. The wipers swished the rain away from her windshield in a fast, steady rhythm. "I'm lost, Dad."

"Lost? Tell me the road you're on and I'll check the internet."

"Harbor Road. But that's not the only reason I called."

Tapping sounded across the line. "H-a-r-b-o-r Road? Let's see where you are."

She smiled into the phone. "You and your computer. What would you do without it?"

"I'd be lost, too. So, what's the other reason you called?"

I'm in love. But, he's shown he doesn't fully trust me. How do I put my heart on the line? The thoughts whirled through her mind, but she said, "I miss you."

"I miss you, too. Ah. Here it is. Have a pen handy?"

Cali wrote the directions back to the main road on the notepad Nick had given her, and told her dad goodbye. She had chickened out. She hadn't been able to tell him how involved she had become with Nick, or how conflicted she felt about it.

Another time, she promised herself. The churning mass of dark clouds overhead hid the sun, but the dimming light still indicated the late hour. She checked the time. One hour until nightfall. She promised Nick she would return before dark, and she intended to keep that promise.

It took Cali twenty minutes to arrive back at the main road. Traffic was light, but the wind gusts had picked up, and she drove with caution. She decided to drop by the cottage and pick up some clothes, just in case they couldn't return for a few days. After another ten minutes, Cali arrived at Nick's cottage. Thankfully, the rain had given her a reprieve, and had let up for a few minutes.

With only a little daylight left, Cali planned to allow herself five minutes to gather her clothes into her duffle bag. The rough waves and strong winds sent sea spray high into the air, and the mist covered her as she climbed the steps to the second story. She tasted salt on her lips as she wiped the dampness from her face, and held back errant strands of hair as the wind whipped them across her eyes.

Cali paused when she reached the top step. Nick had engaged the hurricane protection, blocking access to the door. Determined not to let the barrier keep her from having a fresh set of clothes, she took an extra precious few minutes to crank the slatted material up.

Once she gained entrance, she slipped into the bathroom first, and then packed as fast as she could. By the time she walked back to the living room, darkness had fallen. She peered through the door, and her heart jammed in her chest. The water level had climbed to an alarming level.

Standing close to the sliding glass door, she felt the wind pouring through its cracks. Each crashing wave brought new fears to the surface. She would be trapped if the storm surge crested the sand dunes.

Fearing she had waited too late to leave, Cali paced, wondering what to do. She could head for the car, but would be swept away if the waves toppled the dunes. Was it more dangerous to leave than to stay? Nick had said the cottage had a solid foundation, and if the dunes held she would be safe. But what if the dunes crumbled?

Thunder cracked, making her jump. She had been on edge for so many hours, anxiety had become a constant companion and her head throbbed from the tension. The wind forced the cottage to sway, and Cali made her decision. She grabbed her duffle bag and her purse, heading for the sliding glass door.

Cali peered into the darkness as she neared the door. The furious ocean swells had increased. Her heart lurched in her chest. She fought for breath as a huge wave hurried toward the dunes. The speed of the mound of water both fascinated and terrified her. The dune wouldn't hold much longer under the assault. It could not withstand the force of the wave. In the next instant, and in one sweeping motion, the wave swallowed the pile of sand and surged under the cottage. The cottage trembled upon impact. The stilts creaked under the attack, and the floor vibrated. The lights went out, and panic set in. Cali imagined herself trapped in a sinking ship, with no way out. Fear clutched her, and her breaths became quick and shallow as she slumped to the floor.

She peered out at the ocean as it poured over the molten dunes. Wave after wave now assaulted the cottage. Too late to drive to safety, she had only one thing left she could do.

She searched through her purse, found her cell phone, and dialed Nick's number.

"Cali? Is that you?" His words sounded strained against the howling wind.

He was outside in the storm.

She raised her voice, hoping to get through to him. "The dunes gave away. The water's breaking under your cottage. The foundation's shaking."

"Why are you at the cottage? I asked you to go to the station."

"I came back for my clothes, in case we couldn't get back for a few days."

A muffled curse came through the speaker.

"I'm sorry. I shouldn't have come back here," Cali admitted.

"I'm on the southern shores. I can't get to you fast enough to get you out of there."

"What should I do?"

"Stay inside. The cottage is solid. It'll hold for a while. I'll send someone to get you out and bring you to the station."

"OK."

"Cali?"

"Yeah?"

"Hang in there. I'll see you soon..." he hesitated as if he wanted to say more, but didn't.

****

Shielding the phone from the driving wind the best he could, Nick dialed the station and asked Helen to send Deputy Owen to get Cali out of the swamped cottage. The connection was poor, but Helen repeated his instructions before the call was lost.

Slipping his phone into his pocket, Nick bent his head against the driving rain and concentrated on hauling the yellow barricade across the highway. He had discovered the washed out portion in the nature preserve, and had needed to warn anyone left on the streets not to come this way.

A gust of wind threatened to cast him aside, but he held fast to the warning sign and continued to tug it across the sand-covered asphalt. The waves crashed over the highway in the distance, completely covering it. The high tide wasn't due in for another hour, which meant the storm surge had not reached its peak. Nick's pulse quickened. The flooding would only become worse before getting better.

Lord, please keep everyone safe, he prayed as he worked, a*nd help Deputy Owen get to Cali before it's too late.*

When Nick had secured the road barrier, he ran for his truck and climbed inside. The cab rocked from side to side, but still provided welcome relief from the forceful winds. He removed his hat and wiped the wet, gritty sand from his face, hoping anyone who may attempt to travel this way would use common sense and not try to go around the roadblock. Revving the engine, Nick headed to the station to meet Cali.

Chapter Twenty-Two

Cali stood in front of the door, with damp palms and a racing heart. Lightning flashed, illuminating the night, revealing the immense waves crashing over what was left of the dunes. *Lord, keep this cottage strong. Please let it hold up in the storm.* She closed her eyes, clutching her duffle bag and purse to her chest.

Several long minutes later, a knock sounded on the door. She looked up. A tall, broad-shouldered figure stood in front of the glass, sending the beam of a bright flashlight through the door. Light blinded her as it shined in her face. She winced, shielding her eyes from the assault.

The door cracked open. "Cali, I'm here to help you get out of here."

She didn't recognize the man's voice. She strained to see who it was.

"I'm Chad Livingston. We met on the beach earlier this week." He lowered the flashlight, allowing her to see his shadowed features.

Startled, she stepped back. She had expected Nick to send a deputy, not a lifeguard. Relief flooded through her anyway. She wasn't alone anymore.

He stepped inside and slid the door shut, his clothes dripping puddles of ocean water on the tiled floor, and splattering across her shoes. "What do you say we get out of here?"

"The sooner the better."

"What's in the bag?"

"Clothes."

"Leave them here. There's no way to get yourself and them back to my truck."

"All right," she reluctantly agreed. "But I'm bringing my purse."

"Fair enough. We'll have to wade through the waves. I want you to link your arm in mine and hold on as tight as you can. Ready?"

She tucked her purse against her side. "Yes."

He slid the door open. They had to lean against the wind and fight to stay on their feet. Frightened at the powerful gusts, Cali clung to Chad, leaning on him for support.

The water surge covered the bottom of the steps, submerging the carport by several feet. She prayed Chad would have the strength to carry them through to safety.

He jumped down the last of the steps, pulling her along beside him. Chills ran through her as the water enveloped them up to their waists.

"Look out!" he shouted as a wave barreled into them.

Cali held her purse up just in time to keep it from becoming saturated. They tumbled with the wave, as it carried them farther inland. When the wave receded, they were left in knee-deep water.

"Here comes another. Run!" Chad shouted above the roaring surf.

They scrambled toward the truck, but the wave caught them, tossing them forward, and scraping their exposed skin against the rough cement driveway. Cali swallowed a mouthful of water, and gagged on the cool, salty liquid.

Another wave struck before they stumbled out of the water, both gasping for breath. The scrapes on Cali's knees and shins stung, and her eyes burned from the salt water. When she could speak again, she said, "Thank you. I wouldn't have made it without you."

"No problem. Saving people is what I do."

Emergency lights flashed on top of his red truck, and two Jet Ski's sat ready for action in the back. Chad helped her inside the cab, and then climbed into the driver's seat. Shivers racked Cali's body as her cold, soaked clothes clung to her skin.

Chad turned his green-eyed gaze toward her and flashed a triumphant smile. "You did great, Cali."

"I thought I was going under a few times."

"I wouldn't have let you drown," he said with confidence.

He carefully drove the truck to a wide, white building several blocks away. "This is the headquarters for the Coral Isle Lifeguard and Marine Rescue. Let's go in and get warm. Sound good?"

"Yes, it does," she answered through chattering teeth.

Chad opened the door to the headquarters and led Cali inside. The quiet surprised her. She expected to see the room bustling with activity. She was about to ask why it wasn't, when the phone rang and captured Chad's attention.

He looked completely at ease, as he rested his hip on the desk, talking on the phone. Other than his wet clothes, he showed no indication he had just rescued her from a drowning cottage. Chad's solid voice should have comforted her. But it didn't. Cali needed to hear Nick's voice. She needed to be near him.

Chad hung up and disappeared into an office for a moment. He returned, carrying a white T-shirt. "You need to get into dry clothes. This may be big on you, but it's dry. There's a restroom in my office. You can change there." He pointed to the office he had just been in.

"Thank you."

Cali slipped past him, relieved to have a moment alone to calm her rattled nerves. She found the bathroom and shut the door, but found no lock on it. She leaned against the door, just in case, and switched shirts. Chad's oversized T-shirt stuck to her damp skin, and she pulled at it, trying to keep the cotton from clinging. The faint scent of limes drifted up from the shirt, reminding her of the lime-scented lotion both Chad and Trey had worn at the beach.

She warmed her hands under the faucet and closed her eyes, saying a quick, silent prayer, *Lord, thank you for keeping me safe, and please keep Serena safe, too.* Cold chills ran down her body again, this time with the thought of Serena restrained inside a cottage threatened by the stormy sea.

Thankful to have her wet shirt off, she wrung it out in the sink, then carried it with her back into the main area, and hung it on the back of a chair. Looking across the room, Cali searched for something tangible to focus on, something simple to calm her mounting anxieties.

She studied the layout as Chad picked up another phone call. Three desks occupied the main area, and a few doors led to offices. The faint aroma of coffee permeated the air, probably left over from earlier in the day. A large dry-erase board covered a portion of the white cinderblock wall and she walked over to it. She read the various notes posted on the board. The high temperature was listed as ninety-seven degrees, with the ocean water in the lower eighties. She studied a tidal chart posted in the far right corner.

Chad disconnected the call. After a moment, he stepped near as she studied the information. He pointed to a row of squares. "Each of these squares represents the lifeguard stands. The name written

Night Waves

inside the square is the person assigned to that particular stand for the day."

"Anna told me about the rotating shifts." Nick had too, but she wasn't about to let Chad know he and his staff had been investigated. She felt Chad watching her and lifted her gaze.

"I like Anna. She's young and eager to please me. She does what I tell her to do without question." His gaze roamed over Cali's face and his voice softened. "I like that in a woman."

Her skin crawled. She took a step back, returning her focus to the board.

The phone rang again and he turned to answer it. She listened as Chad explained the shelters remained open, but all emergency services had been shut down and the caller had to wait out the storm. She shivered at the thought of people in the hurricane needing help, and not having access to it. And yet, Nick was still out there, doing what he could to help anyone in need.

Cali's gaze roamed the board, for no other reason than to keep her mind focused. Then, her gaze landed on the top right corner. It listed the date as Tuesday's date, not today's. She had met Anna, Trey and Chad on that day.

According to the schedule, Anna was assigned to station three. But, Cali had met her at station number five. Trey had been assigned to station one. But, Cali had met him at station six.

Something was wrong.

As she studied the chart, the door opened and Trey walked in. The blustery wind scattered papers and the rain pelted through the door. After shutting the storm out, he looked from Cali to Chad and asked, "What are you still doing here? They've ordered an evacuation of the island." He pulled a raincoat off, shaking it before hanging it up. "Everyone else has left."

"Just tying up loose ends," Chad said as he held

his hand over the phone's mouthpiece.

Trey strode over to Cali. "You're drenched. Are you OK?"

"Yes. Chad rescued me from Sheriff Justice's cottage. The sand dune gave way and the tide swept under the cottage. We had to wade through several feet of waves. I was terrified the entire structure was going to fall into the ocean."

"It's dangerous out there. That's why I'm surprised you're still on the island."

"I didn't want to leave Serena."

"Serena?"

Cali tensed. Trey knew exactly who she was referring to. She had shown Serena's picture to him, and he had been at the press conference. So why act as if he couldn't place her?

"Serena Taylor."

"Oh. That's right. She's the friend of yours that went missing. She hasn't turned up yet?"

Cali shook her head as wariness crept over her. "Not yet." She glanced away and pointed to the board. "Chad was explaining that these squares represent the lifeguard stands, and the names of the lifeguards are posted here for each shift. Right?" Cali asked as if she hadn't understood Chad's explanation.

"That's right. But, the names don't mean much since we switch so many times."

"Switch?"

"Yeah." He ran a hand through his dripping, red hair. "We start out at our assigned locations, but we don't stay there all day."

"What do you mean?"

"We switch stations every so often. Just...you know, to keep from getting bored."

Cali's muscles tensed. "Are these changes recorded?"

"Nah." Trey shrugged. "Why?"

"No reason. Just wondering." Cali attempted to

hide the wave of fear Trey's information had slammed into her.

Nick had cleared the lifeguards as suspects because their shifts hadn't corresponded with where the women had been located on the island. But what if he hadn't known about the multiple, unrecorded shift changes?

As doubts filled her, a memory stilled her movements. Nancy Chandler had mentioned smelling Margaritas. Chad's suntan lotion smelled like limes, and so did his T-shirt. Which very well could have been the source of Nancy's memory. But then, Trey also wore the lotion.

It can't be.

Margaritas and lime. The lifeguard rotation shifts Nick had checked out were bogus. Cali's fear turned into full-blown terror. She was trapped in a storm with two men. One of whom could be a serial rapist.

Chapter Twenty-Three

Nick walked into the station, pulling the door shut against the harsh winds and removing his hat. The emergency lights had activated, telling him the station had lost its power. Helen stood behind her desk wringing her hands. Deputy Owen stepped out of the back hallway with soggy clothes, wet hair and a deep crease edged in his brow.

Nick's gut clenched. He didn't see Cali. He paused in the entrance. "Where is she?"

Owen said, "I went to your cottage…"

"And?" Nick's impatient voice betrayed his growing anxiety.

"And I couldn't find her."

"Did you go inside? I told her to wait there."

"Of course. She wasn't there. But, her car was. It was floating in the surf. I checked inside it, just in case." His voice lowered. "It was empty."

Nick pulled out his cell phone, dialed Cali's number and listened to the voice mail pick up. Her phone was turned off. Why would she turn off her cell phone? He looked at Owen. "Did you call out to her?"

"I used the spare key you told me about before. I searched the whole place, including your level. She was gone, Sheriff."

Nick's heart plummeted. Fear gripped him. But

instead of immobilizing him, his protective instincts kicked in. He reached for his hat, ready to go and search.

"Sheriff, I know you're not heading back out into the storm," Helen's southern drawl held a warning to it.

"I have to find her," he said with conviction.

Helen paused, and then gave a reluctant nod. Owen took a step forward.

"You stay here." Nick held out a hand. "Call me if Cali shows up."

Nick drove as fast as the conditions allowed. Trees bent and swayed with the high winds. Several cracked branches dangled precariously over the roadway, while others had completely fallen, stretching across the pavement.

He prayed he would be able to weave through the destruction to the cottage, and he prayed he would discover a clue as to where Cali had gone. There was a chance she hadn't heard Deputy Owen calling. A slight chance, but still a chance, and as long as there was hope, he refused to give up.

As Nick continued to drive, he strained to see through the thick downpour of rain. He passed by another vehicle, dodging broken limbs and road signs. He wanted to stop and force the driver to seek shelter, but could not afford to take the time. Everyone had been warned, an evacuation had been ordered. He could not control what people did, no matter how reckless.

He jumped when something slammed into his truck. He glanced through the side mirror. A beach chair was pinned against the door by the wind. A moment later, the red trimmed chair bounced to the road then tumbled into a storefront, crashing through an unprotected window.

Nick prayed no one was inside.

It took him three times longer than usual to drive to the cottage. He had to detour around a flooded section of the roadway, and avoid several fallen trees. At one point, he drove over a battered stop sign, which had crashed to the ground. When he finally caught sight of his home, fear lodged in his throat and dread filled his heart.

Several feet of roaring surf had engulfed his carport. Waves crashed into the stilts, battering the cottage's foundation. He parked the truck at a safe distance and stepped out. He cringed as the cottage groaned from the storm's relentless assault.

"Stay with me, baby," he whispered, speaking both to the cottage and to Cali.

He removed his pistol from his ankle holster, his wallet from his pocket and deposited them in the truck. Ducking, he headed for the devastating waves, preparing to combat the force of the rising tide.

****

Cali fought hard to control her breathing. She fumbled with the neckline on the T-shirt she wore, hoping to disguise her racing pulse. As Nick had pointed out, the soft spot at the base of her neck gave away her hidden emotions.

She itched to get out of the lime-scented material. The moment she had begun to suspect Chad, the soft cotton had turned abrasive against her skin. She wished she could take it off, but it would appear suspicious.

Trey stood next to her, taller than she remembered. His biceps strained against his short sleeves as he crossed his arms and studied her. "You seem interested in how things work around here. Why is that?"

She shrugged, pretending indifference. "It comes with being a reporter." *Could Trey have Serena locked away somewhere?* Her suspicions grew with each passing moment, making her leery of every move he made.

Chad's footsteps sounded behind her. "I'm

heading out. I'll give you a lift if you want."

Trey spoke quickly, "I'm on my way out, too. I'll give you a ride." He stepped closer, his gaze flickering over her.

Cali looked between the two, wondering if she could make a right choice. Maybe they were both involved.

Chad lifted his shoulders. "It's up to you, Cali."

She studied the two men. Neither appeared anxious or foreboding. Neither looked like a serial rapist. She began to wonder if she had overreacted. But, she still didn't want to go anywhere with either of them. "I don't want to be any trouble. I'll call Sheriff Justice. He'll pick me up."

Trey glanced at his watch. "I'd better get going then. I'll see you around." He nodded at Chad then looked at Cali. "Be careful out there." He picked up his raingear and headed out the door, leaving Cali alone with Chad.

Indecision immobilized her. Should she catch up with Trey? What if he was the stalker? What about Chad? What if neither of them was to blame?

"I'll drop you off anywhere you want."

"I'm sure Nick can come and get me." She reached for her purse.

Chad stepped forward. "No need. I'm heading past the sheriff's station anyway. I could have you there in a few minutes. It's no trouble."

Cali studied Chad's guileless expression. Maybe she had overreacted. "You don't mind?"

"Not at all. I'll grab my things and we'll get going."

Cali swung her purse over her shoulder, picked up the wet shirt she had draped over a chair, and waited. When he had gathered his things he headed for the door, and she followed.

"Let me pull the truck close to the door for you so you won't have to get drenched again." He ran into the storm, bending low against the harsh winds.

Chad wasn't behaving like a criminal. Cali began to feel foolish at her assumptions. A moment later, he pulled a dark-green Jeep Cherokee close to the door, opening the passenger side for her. Cali ran through the torrential rain. She climbed in, grateful he had driven so close. "Thanks."

"No problem. I'll lock up and we'll get going." He climbed out, leaving the engine running.

The lime scent assaulted her again, causing her doubts to return. For a split second, she considered locking Chad out and taking his Jeep. Then common sense made her hesitate. What would she tell Nick? She had become anxious and committed grand theft auto? Not wanting to become a felon, she tried to calm her jittery nerves and took deep, calming breaths.

Cali glanced around the interior. Dust covered the dashboard and air vents. A bottle of lotion sat in the floorboard along with a few discarded fast food containers.

Chad slammed back into the jeep in a hurry, bringing a splattering of rain with him. He ran a hand through his wet hair. "Whew. It's getting bad out there."

"Yes it is. I'm sure Nick's getting worried about where we are. I should call him." She unzipped her purse.

"Why do you keep mentioning Nick? He's not here. He's not the one who saved you," Chad's voice had a new edge to it. He shifted his hands on the wheel and pulled out onto the road.

Cali's hand stilled as she swallowed a lump forming in her throat. "He would've come, but he was too far away. That's why he called you to come for me."

A tight smile formed at the edge of his lips. "I never said he called me."

Cali's suspicions deepened and a chill ran down her spine. "But he said he'd send someone…"

"Well." Chad sighed as he turned down a debris-filled road. He took his time answering as he maneuvered around a large tree branch, which had broken and filled half of the roadway. Once past the obstacle, he pressed the gas pedal. "I came for you. But not because of him."

The hair on the back of Cali's neck stood on end. "How did you know I needed help?" She tried to sound calm and unaware.

"I didn't."

Her vision narrowed as shock stole her breath. "But then, w-why did you come?"

His kept his head facing forward, but his gaze slid to her. "I came for you Cali." His voice lowered, taking her fear to a new level.

"How did you know where to find me? I only met you once." She had to ask, although terrified of the answer.

He sighed. "You have too many questions. Relax, Cali. We're going to have plenty of time to get to know each other."

She ignored his strange comment, distracted by the left turn he made. "You're going the wrong way. The sheriff's station is east of here."

"We won't be going there."

Her eyes widened. Her pulse raced. She had to get out. Now.

God, grant me courage...

She released her seatbelt and attacked the lock on the door, flipping it as fast as she could. She jerked the door handle and shoved the door open. The pavement went by in a blur, and she braced herself for impact. Chad's hand gripped her arm. Desperation filled her. She pulled against him, ignoring the pain streaking through her flesh.

He slowed the Jeep to a stop. "Don't you want to see your friend again, Cali?"

Shock paralyzed her.

The strength of the wind ripped the door handle

from her grasp, forcing it to open wide. Sharp pain struck her fingers, instantly numbing them and rendering them useless. Rain assaulted her, and wind-blown sand blasted her face, her eyes and ears. Cali turned to shield herself from the onslaught, and came face to face with Chad. He leaned over her, reaching for the door. The lime scent he carried with him sickened her. His large biceps strained against the forces of nature, but he managed to shut the door in one sweeping movement.

He remained close, leaning across her. The raging storm threatened from the outside, and Chad's presence threatened from within. The Jeep shifted with a gust of wind, and then rocked back into place. An electrical transformer blew, sending sparks flying into the air. Cali turned just in time to see a thick, black power line disengage and slice through the air like an uncontrolled whip. It landed a few feet from the Jeep, sparking and hissing as it touched the flooded street. Cali instinctively drew away from the door, afraid to touch anything metal in the car.

Chad remained unaffected by the incident. He inched back, his eyes sliding down the length of her. Assessing. Gauging. But, with no real interest. What his gaze did reveal terrified her. Darkness swelled to the surface, cloaking his once-friendly green eyes with violent intent.

Given the choice, Cali would rather take her chances outside in the hurricane than remain stuck inside the Jeep with Chad. But, any further escape attempts must be delayed. The downed power line made any immediate attempts potentially deadly. She would have to look for another avenue of escape.

Chad straightened in his seat. "Now that I have your attention, I know you'll cooperate."

"Where is Serena?"

"You don't need to worry about her."

"Is she OK? Did you hurt her?"

"This isn't about her anymore. It's about you and me."

"What do you want from me?"

"Serena hasn't seen my face. None of them have." He pulled his shoulders back, puffing out his chest as if proud of his accomplishment as he resumed driving.

"I've seen you..." Cali's words trailed off, and she wished she hadn't pointed out the fact.

"It doesn't matter."

"W-why?"

"Because I intend to keep you." The muscles in his arms flexed as he spun the steering wheel, avoiding another fallen obstacle.

An intense fear clawed its way up through her chest, tightened it, making it hard to breathe. "Why me?"

"You're special."

Cali's stomach dropped and nausea rolled through her. "Nick will find me."

Without warning, he grabbed her hair and jerked her toward him. Pain erupted, and she felt as if he had yanked a wad of hair from her scalp. His gaze seared into hers. "Not if he thinks you're dead."

"You won't get away. He'll track you down. He'll hunt you." She held her eyes steady on his, refusing to give in to the terror.

His narrowed eyes bore down on her. "You have too much faith in him."

Nick's words rushed back. *We have limits. God doesn't.* "You're wrong. I do trust Nick, but I put my faith in God."

"How nice for you. But, you're in my hands now Cali." He gave her hair a tug, exemplifying his point.

She wished Chad would stop using her name. Every time he did, a new wave of shivers ran down her arms. "No. I'm always in God's hands."

"We'll see if you still think so in a few days." He released his hold on her hair, putting his hand back on the steering wheel. She inched away, rubbing her scalp in an effort to ease the pain.

"You left Serena's necklace in my motel room," she said. "Why didn't you take me then?"

"I needed to prepare for you."

"Prepare?"

"I needed time to get rid of Serena and Marlene first. To make room."

Her blood ran cold. "Get rid of?"

"That's right."

"Where did you take them?"

"Take a guess. I'm the High Tide Stalker, remember?"

Cali trembled. "A-are they...alive?"

"I'm growing tired of your questions." His gaze narrowed, and his knuckles turned white against the wheel.

Afraid to provoke him further, she fell into silence.

A few minutes passed as Chad concentrated on weaving his way through the streets. Cali tried to note the turns, and any other recognizable places. They passed through residential neighborhoods where the wind had battered roofs, pulling shingles free and tearing eaves apart. A few streetlights still glowed several blocks down, but only blackout conditions prevailed in the direction they headed.

The darkness, combined with the blustery wind and driving rain, made it nearly impossible to make out any street names. She caught a few letters here and there, but nothing that fully described their location. He took so many turns, Cali wondered if he was trying to confuse her.

She had to tell Nick about Chad before it was too late. Cali's eyes strayed to her opened purse.

"I took your cell phone."

She jumped, surprised he had noticed her intent. She dug inside her purse. The phone was gone. "When?"

"When you went into the bathroom to change." He pulled the thin, silver phone out of his back pocket and tapped it on the steering wheel. "You'll learn soon that I'm not stupid, Cali."

She lunged for the phone. He lifted his arm and used his elbow to shove her back. "This kind of behavior will not be tolerated," he said as if he had full authority over her.

"It doesn't matter. Nick will find me." Cali believed her words, but prayed it wouldn't be too late when he did. "He'll make you pay for what you've done."

"Enough." Chad lifted his hand as if to strike her.

She recoiled, holding up her shaky hands.

"That's better. What do you say we give your boyfriend Nick a call? Want to say goodbye?"

Cali's pulse increased. If given the chance to speak with him, all she would have to do is say Chad's name, and Nick would be able to find her. Her hopes rose.

"On second thought, I think I'll do the talking," he said as if he had read her mind. He glanced at her, studying her reaction.

"You never planned on letting me say a word did you?"

Chad smirked as he pulled into a driveway in front of a small yellow, wind-battered cottage. He cut the engine, flipped open her phone, and turned it on. When it was ready, he dialed a number.

Chad clamped his free hand over Cali's mouth and yanked her head back against his shoulder. His damp, gritty palm felt like wet sandpaper against her skin, and the acrid scent of salty sweat reeked from his body.

He leaned his head close. So close, she heard Nick's voice as he answered, "Cali? Where are you?"

Chapter Twenty-Four

"Sorry. Cali can't talk right now." A man's voice interrupted Nick's initial relief. "Then again, I'm not so sorry."

Nick recognized the stalker's voice from when he had called before. Fear clawed through his chest. His heartbeat skipped, and then jumped into overdrive. "Where is she? If you hurt her..."

"I thought you might like to say bye to your woman. Here she is."

Muffled screams tore through the phone. The gut wrenching sound confirmed Nick's worst fears. The High Tide Stalker had taken Cali.

"Release her," Nick demanded. Cold sweat beaded across his brow. He paced across the upper level of his cottage as it creaked and shuddered with the crash of the surf below.

"You ask for too much. I've released Serena and Marlene. I think that's a fair trade. Don't you?"

"Let me talk to her."

"Don't you think you'd better find the other women before the tide does?"

"I said, let me talk to her," his sharp words evoked a response from Cali. Another muffled cry came through. "Cali! Stay strong baby. I'll find you," he raised his voice, hoping she would hear him.

A short, jeering laugh taunted Nick. "You'd

better find the other women. How would it look if the famed sheriff of Coral Isle let two women drown in order to save another?"

"Where are they?"

A shout, followed by cursing pierced Nick's ears. Cali screamed, and the line went dead.

"No. Dear God. No," Nick barely recognized his own, hollow voice as he prayed.

He shrugged into his rain jacket, simultaneously dialing the station. "Helen, the stalker released two victims. Send Deputies Owen and Castle to the nature preserve. Tell them to be prepared for flooded roads, and tell them not to come back without the women."

"What's your location, Sheriff?"

He hesitated. "The High Tide Stalker took Cali."

Silence filled the airwaves.

"I'm going to find her."

****

"You'll learn to submit." Chad's confident statement surrounded Cali as he forced her out of the Jeep. She fought him, knowing if he got her inside the cottage, her chances of escape would severely diminish. He tossed her cell phone into the back of the Jeep and used both arms to throw her over his shoulder.

Cali beat his back with her fists. She kicked her legs and hit something solid. He groaned and dropped her to the ground. She landed hard. Pain coursed through her as she fought for breath. Chad loomed over her and raised his hand. She twisted and struggled to her feet. He grabbed her shoulder, spinning her around with his harsh grip. She turned her head and sunk her teeth into his hand.

Cali tasted blood.

Repulsed, she pulled her teeth from his flesh. He kicked her feet out from under her, causing her to fall. The wind blew debris into her eyes, and she closed them against the pain. He again tossed her over his shoulder in one swift movement. She flailed her arms and legs, trying to knock him off balance. She screamed as loud as she could, but the winds muffled her desperate cries for help.

"Stop fighting me. You're no match for my strength," he said as he carried her the remaining distance to the cottage. He unlocked and opened the door. She latched onto the doorframe, digging her fingers into the wood.

Her attempts slowed his progress, but didn't stop him. He tore her hands lose with a violent jerk, and dragged her inside, tossing his keys into a nearby container. When he shut the door, darkness consumed the damp, musty room and instantly awakened her claustrophobia. The smell of rotting food assaulted her senses, and she gagged in reflex. Panic tore through her, renewing her strength to fight. She jerked back and fell off his shoulder and onto the floor, but he had her by the arm in an instant. She yanked and pulled at his grip as she struggled to catch the breath she had lost on impact with the hard floor. A warm trickle of his blood rolled down her skin.

At least when she had bitten him, she had done some damage.

He grunted, and then a metallic chink awakened her imagination. *What is he doing?* At a severe disadvantage in the dark, she had no idea where to turn for help. She groped for a weapon with one arm, while he continued to yank on her other arm. Then a hard, cold band clamped around her wrist. When it clicked closed, she ceased to fight. Chad had managed to handcuff her to something unmovable.

He stepped away, stumbled and cursed again. A moment later, the flame from a match lit the room. He lit a candle. Then another. By the time he had finished, a dozen candles flickered in a living room and kitchen.

Large stacks of newspapers littered the brown-carpeted floor. Dust covered the coffee and end tables. Several leftover pizza boxes lay scattered in the kitchen, and food rotted on dirtied dishes on the counter, obviously the source of the putrid smell.

Cali tugged at her manacled wrist, discovering she was cuffed to the bar that separated the living room from the kitchen.

Chad looked at his bloody hand. His gaze crept up. "You'll be sorry you bit me."

Alarm surged through her. Searching for a way to avoid his revenge, she asked, "Why? Why did you take them?"

He rubbed a hand across his jaw, making the stubble rasp beneath his touch. "Let's see." He sat on the edge of a futon sofa, which was the only place to sit in the small space. "I took Nancy because she back-talked me. I will not tolerate that." A satisfied smirk tilted his lips. "She learned her lesson."

"The others?"

"The kid sassed me, too."

"I know Serena didn't. She's not like that."

"No. She's not. I took her because I could."

Cali lifted her eyebrows. "Because you could? That's the only reason?" She adjusted her arm to ease the burning pain. He had pulled so hard to get her inside, she was afraid a muscle might have torn in her shoulder, or worse.

He shrugged. "Serena was convenient. An easy target. She wasn't paying attention to her surroundings, so I chose her. But, I had no need for her after I met you. I saw you talking with Trey, and I knew you were next."

Cali swallowed the bile rising in her throat. "Next? Do you ever plan on stopping?"

"Especially after you called me a coward at the press conference," he continued as if she hadn't spoken. "That was a mistake, for you. For me, it was an awakening."

"Because you know it's true?" she dared ask.

He sat forward. "No. Because I was growing bored with the others, and I didn't understand why until I saw you. I knew you'd provide a challenge the others didn't. I'm going to enjoy breaking your spirit. You'll learn to control your mouth. You'll learn to obey me. You'll see." A glimmer of perversion entered his eyes.

Cali remembered what Nick had said about the perpetrator needing to take more risks in order to satisfy his growing need for power and control. Discovering how accurate he had been was turning out to be a nightmare.

"Did you take Serena from the beach?" Somehow, Cali couldn't imagine Chad carrying her, kicking and screaming from the populated area. "Or did you drug her like you did the other women?"

He tapped his index finger on his cheek. "You are a curious one aren't you? I suspected you would be, since you're a reporter." He hesitated, and a gloating smile appeared. "I saw Serena on the beach. I followed her back to her cottage. Just like the others. Of course, the sheriff delayed my plans for you. Always hanging around..." he waved a hand in the air with disgust. "Then he took you from the motel. It cost me precious time to locate you. But, the newspaper helped me a great deal with that." He sighed, long and deep, his shoulders heaving with the effort. "No matter. You're mine now."

A chill of revulsion plagued her, but Cali refused to be sidetracked. "Did you break into their cottages like you did my motel room?"

"Twice. Once to lace their drinks with GHB, the second to retrieve them after they'd passed out." He looked pleased with himself.

"So, you target unsuspecting women who are alone and take them after they've been drugged? You are the worst kind of coward."

He rose and stalked toward her. "You'll learn

not to use that word, Cali." He traced a finger along her chin, his breath hot on her cheek. "Soon enough."

She jerked away, moving as far away as her restraints allowed. "Why did you bother to take Marlene if you wanted me next?" she asked, trying to distract him.

"To lure the sheriff away from you. I would've had you last night, if Sheriff Justice hadn't returned at the wrong time."

"You were outside my cottage last night?"

"Don't you mean *Nick's* cottage?" he sneered.

"I don't understand why. You have a good career. You save people for a living. Why jeopardize it to hurt women?"

"I'm a complex man, Cali. There's much more to me than what people see on the outside. I have friends, family. I can get a date whenever I want. But none of them satisfy my deepest needs."

A shiver swept through her. "There are people out there who can help you."

"I know." His eyes strayed to her. "You're one of them. Hungry?"

His unexpected question threw her off guard. Cali studied him in the glow of the candlelight. The yellow, dancing flames cast shadows across his unpredictable features. He stepped back and walked around the counter to the kitchen as if nothing were out of the ordinary.

"Let me help you prepare something." She would try anything to get out of the handcuffs.

Chad stopped, turned and walked back. "I told you I'm not stupid."

Cali's mind threaded through possible replies. *How can I convince him?* If she were to get free, he could easily overcome her physically. The words she had spoken to Serena at the press conference came back. *Fight back and fight hard.* Cali had been speaking in physical terms at the time. But now, she would have to fight with another means.

God, grant me serenity...

She would have to calm her nerves and focus if she was going to talk her way out of the cuffs. Cali took a deep breath and let it out slowly. "Why don't you let me go? You said I'm no match for your strength. And you're right. You're a strong man, Chad. I could never overcome you."

"I know," he agreed.

"I'll do what you say."

Chad made no attempt to release her. "You're not ready to submit to me yet. Don't play games, Cali. You'll get burned."

She switched tactics. "What's the matter? Don't think you can handle me?" she taunted, turning her false submission into aggression.

He laughed a humorless crackle of a sound. "You're nothing for me to worry about."

"If you really believe that, uncuff me."

Chad clenched his jaw, appearing to consider her words.

She took a chance and added, "Or do you want me to see what kind of coward you really are?" She braced for his reaction.

"Don't call me that!" Angry lines formed across his brow, his face reddened, and his pulse throbbed at his temple. He removed the key from his pocket.

He jerked her wrist toward him and jammed the key into the slot. Within seconds, he had her wrist free. He took her arm, twisting the already painful muscles as he drew her near. "I told you not to call me a coward. You will regret your decision to disobey me."

Desperate, Cali tugged against him, looking for an opportunity to escape. Chad forced her toward the futon, the handcuffs clanking along the way. He shoved her onto the thin cushion, holding her wrist. If he confined her again, she would have no chance to escape, no chance to find Serena, and no chance to see if she and Nick could have a future together. A surge of adrenaline and anger swept through her system. No one had the right to jeopardize her future or her happiness.

Chad could bind her again within seconds. Cali searched the room for a weapon and spotted a wide brimmed candle within reach. She took her free hand, grabbed the candle and shoved it at his face. The melted wax sprayed across his exposed skin and splattered across his eyes. Adhering. Burning.

He screeched, releasing her wrist to cover his face with his palms.

Cali leapt away, grabbing another candle. But instead of throwing it at him, she tossed the candle into the pile of newspapers on the floor.

The paper ignited and the carpet caught fire, spreading as if fueled by gasoline. Flames engulfed the room within seconds. Smoke choked her lungs. She dropped to her knees, gasping for breath. She crawled to the door and opened it. She looked back. Chad stood, reaching out, groping the air in blind fury.

Cali ran into the raging storm, leaving the door open wide, desperate to escape the man who had become known as the High Tide Stalker. Adrenaline gave her momentum, but fear made her clumsy. She tripped as fear clawed at her, making her flight reckless with abandon. She climbed to her feet, determined to fight her way to freedom.

The wind tossed her around as if she weighed no more than a child. She fell again, struggled to her feet and ran. She squinted against the debris-filled wind and held up her arms to shield her face.

She ran toward the dark outline of a neighboring cottage, darting into the side yard and around the corner of a shadowy screened-in porch. Wind chimes clanked nearby, and tree branches scraped against windows. She backed against the cottage, plastering herself against the wooden shingles as the rain pelted her in a relentless cascade.

Gasping for air, she fell to her knees, shivering as her soaked clothes clung to her skin. With teeth chattering, Cali dared to peek around the corner. Flames had already eaten a hole through the roof on Chad's cottage, and the front door remained open wide, swinging back and forth in the wind. The orange-yellow glow of the fire illuminated the doorway. But she didn't see Chad. Was he still inside? Bile rose in her throat. Even forced to defend herself, the reality of someone in pain because of her actions made her nauseous.

She needed a phone. She needed Nick.

Only God can fulfill all of our needs, she remembered Nick's words. She prayed, "Help me Lord. Protect me."

She searched for signs of life in the neighborhood. But, with no electricity, she had no way of telling if anyone remained behind in the storm. Afraid to run into the open and knock on doors, she remained hunched beside the cottage, praying someone would see the flames and call for help. Then she remembered Chad telling one of the callers at the station that no emergency help was available due to the mandatory evacuation. Her heart lurched, and her hopes of finding help faded.

She peeked around the cottage again, and her breath caught. Chad had found his way outside. Flames danced on his clothes, and he dropped to the ground and rolled. The drenched ground doused the fire, and he climbed to his feet. He spun in circles, holding his arms open wide. "I'll find you Cali. And when I do..." He laughed, a deep and sinful sound erupting from his throat. "You'll wish you never laid eyes on Coral Isle."

The firelight illuminated his contorted features. One eye was swollen shut, but the other was open. From the way Chad swept his head from side to side in search of her, Cali knew she had not blinded him after all. She stood on wobbly knees and braced herself as Chad began to head across his front yard. Soon, he would be where he could see her. She turned and ran, tears blinding her vision as much as the wind and rain. She ducked behind the cottage, and then stopped.

She needed to think. She needed a plan. Running in blind fear would only get her caught again.

God grant me wisdom...

Cali took in her surroundings, looking for a weapon. The burning cottage illuminated a pile of firewood in Chad's back yard. She contemplated grabbing a log and using it for defense. But what if he took it and used it against her? Chad could inflict major damage, and she didn't want to provide the tools for him to use.

Afraid she would be caught any minute, she circled around the back, and stepped toward Chad's burning cottage. He wouldn't expect her to return there. She hoped.

Cali had to get help. She remembered Chad tossing her cell phone in the back of his Jeep. Had he locked the doors?

Her heart raced with hope, and fear. She had to try.

She broke into a full run, shielding her face from the overwhelming heat from the fire. As she approached his Jeep, a sharp, guttural sound erupted from somewhere behind her. She leapt for the door, afraid to turn around and look. The door was unlocked.

She pulled it open and jumped inside, dark, acrid smoke following her in. She choked on the polluted air, coughing and gasping for breath. She swung the door toward her, but a large hand blocked the way. Chad had caught up with her.

Ice-cold fear shocked her system, threatening to immobilize her. Her survival instincts kicked in, and she yanked the door back again as hard as she could. The door bounced on its hinges as it crushed Chad's hand.

He screamed, pulling back to cradle his injury.

Cali shut the door completely. She scrambled for the lock, and pressed the button. The locks engaged just in time to keep him from gaining entrance. His face appeared in the window, the firelight reflecting the fury burning in his gaze. She glanced at the cottage, wondering if he would be able to get back inside and retrieve the keys to the Jeep.

Chad slammed his elbow into the window. Cali recoiled and lunged in the back for the cell phone. Desperation tore through her when she didn't see it on the seat. Then, a split second later, she found it on the floorboard.

Cali directed her thoughts to one person. She opened the phone and dialed, praying he would answer.

Chapter Twenty-Five

Nick's palms slid across the steering wheel, damp from worry. In all his years in law enforcement, he had never faced a fear as all-consuming as this one. He couldn't contemplate losing Cali, not now when he had just found her.

Flashes of lightning illuminated black smoke billowing in the night sky. He turned on his emergency lights, and took the next right, heading for the source.

His cell phone rang.

"Justice," he answered.

"Nick..."

Momentarily shocked to hear Cali's voice, he hesitated before asking, "Cali. Baby, where are you?"

"It's C-Chad. The lifeguard. He's..." A loud crack sounded, and then her scream erupted through the phone.

Terror sliced through him. "Cali. Cali!"

"He's going to get in. Hurry Nick. I can't stop him."

"Where did he take you?"

"His cottage."

He remembered the address from when he was investigating the possibility of the lifeguards as suspects. "Hang in there. Use everything you've got to fight him. I'm on my way." Another scream erupted, tearing through his core.

"I set his cottage on fire."

His heart throbbed painfully in his chest. His gaze darted to the black smoke billowing through the dark sky, and he realized he was already heading in the right direction. "Are you inside the cottage?"

"N-no. Nick, he's getting in..."

"In where?"

The line went dead. He punched the gas pedal, tearing through broken limbs and driving over fallen obstacles in the road. His tires squealed as he rounded a corner, and his jaw clenched in determination.

Dread compounded with fear as he entered the residential neighborhood. He slammed his foot on the brake pedal and parked a safe distance away from the burning cottage. Although the heavy rain combated the flames, the gusty winds fueled them, kicking them high into the air.

An explosion shattered windows on the right side, sending shards of glass flying in all directions. Black smoke erupted from the new escape route, making the raging fire appear lopsided inside the small, charred cottage.

"She's not inside." Nick reminded himself, as the fiery outburst raged out of control.

One vehicle sat in the driveway, and a man lay sprawled on the ground a few feet away as if he had been thrown aside by the explosion. Then, he stood and limped toward the vehicle. He raised his foot, bashing it into the window.

The outline of a person inside, hunkering against the far side jolted Nick's heart. Cali was inside.

Nick retrieved his pistol, stepped outside and aimed the weapon. "Sheriff's department. Get on the ground!"

The man turned. The flames illuminated his

battered features, and reflections from the flashing blue lights on Nick's truck wound across his face. One eye was swollen, his face streaked with dark ashes. He stood, arms and feet spread wide, ready to fight.

"Don't do it, Livingston." Nick held his pistol in a firm grip as he stepped closer.

Cali erupted from the other side of the vehicle, coughing, falling to her knees. "Nick." Her voice barely carried across the howling wind.

"Cali, get in my truck." He kept his eyes trained on Chad. "Get down, Livingston!"

Cali stumbled past Nick, climbing into his truck to safety.

Chad watched her. A full minute passed before his shoulders slumped. He raised his hands and laced them on the back of his head. He dropped to his knees, glaring in Cali's direction. The cold contempt in his gaze injected a new round of adrenaline into Nick's veins, and he stepped forward, ready to put an end to the High Tide Stalker's crime spree.

****

Cali could not stop shaking. Her drenched clothes stuck to her skin, and her hair lay plastered across her shoulders in a wet, tangled mess. She rubbed her right shoulder where Chad had injured her by dragging her around.

Nick handcuffed Chad and pulled him to his feet. The cruel gaze Chad directed at her chilled her further as Nick walked him toward the truck.

Cali's stomach dropped. Chad had to ride with them.

Dread filled her. Goose bumps covered her skin, and her shaking grew worse. She swallowed the lump forming in her throat.

Nick stopped Chad a few feet from the truck. He turned and faced the man who had stalked the women of Coral Isle for months, and said something

Cali couldn't hear.

Chad shook his head as a devious grin parted his lips.

Then Nick stepped closer, grabbed Chad's T-shirt and yanked him up until they were eye to eye. Nick said a few more words, and then Chad's face fell. Chad spoke again before Nick finally released him.

Nick opened the door and deposited Chad into the backseat. The seatbelt clicked as Nick secured him. Cali had expected Chad to fight, shout and curse. But, he remained still and silent, watching her with deadly intent. She didn't like him being so near, but Nick wouldn't let him hurt her.

She turned and faced the burning cottage. A portion of the roof had collapsed, leaving a gaping hole for the flames to escape. Soon, there would be nothing left. A hollow ache emerged inside her, thinking of the heartache this man had caused, and at how so many lives would be changed forever.

Serena's life would never be the same. Neither would hers.

Anger replaced her sense of relief. Chad had done enough damage. It was time to put an end to his savagery.

As Nick climbed into the driver's seat, she twisted, boldly facing Chad. "Where is she?"

Nick placed a hand on her sore shoulder. She winced, pulling back, but kept her focus on Chad. "I said, where is she?" she yelled.

"Hold on, Cali." Nick's soft voice made her pause. His gaze darted to her shoulder. "Did he hurt you?"

She shrugged glancing at his left shoulder. "I guess I've learned my limitations now, too."

"You did great Cali." Warmth mixed with relief in his smile.

"But it's not over yet." She focused on Chad again, lifting to her knees, ready to climb over the seat and shake the information out of him, now that Nick was there to protect her.

"Cali, look at me," Nick demanded, his voice turning firm.

She heard him, but didn't want to comply. "He knows, Nick. He knows where they are."

He wrapped his hand behind her neck, directing her gaze to his. "I know where they are. Turn around and buckle up."

"You do?"

"Now, Cali."

His no-nonsense demeanor captured her attention. She clicked her seatbelt into place as he put the truck in Drive and made a U-turn in the middle of the street. He lifted the radio handset and contacted Helen at the station.

"Tell the deputies to look for the women three miles into the nature preserve. They're on the inland side of the highway. I'm on my way. I've got the suspect in custody."

"Is Cali OK?" Helen asked.

Nick spared a quick glance at her. "I've got her too. She's shaken, but she's going to be fine."

That remains to be seen, Cali thought. *Depending on whether or not we find Serena in time.*

Nick concentrated on the road as he drove. The wind continued to batter the island, and the rain flooded the streets as the gutters filled to capacity.

"You're shaking." He glanced at her with concern creasing his brow. He reached for her hand, taking it in his warm grasp. "We're almost there."

"How do you know where Serena is?" Cali voiced her fears, daring to look back at Chad, who had lapsed into silence.

He lifted his head a notch. "He told me."

"How can you believe him?"

Chad broke into the conversation. "Because he has no other choice." A smug smile formed at the corner of his lips. "I'm still in control, Cali."

She ignored his comment, turning her full attention back to Nick.

"You'll have to trust me on this one, baby." He glanced her way. His eyes held something more than concern now. Vulnerability showed through, reminding her of when he had asked her to pray with him.

Then the truth hit her. He was acting on instincts, and faith. Not only on what Chad had told him.

"I trust you," she offered in a whisper.

A smile tugged at the corners of his lips, and relief showed in his eyes. Nick pulled onto the highway that ran along the length of the nature preserve. He set the headlight beams to high, and the rays of light reflected the rain as it poured from the sky.

"The road washed out about five miles down. I set up a barrier earlier this evening. But, we should still be able to get as far in as we need to."

Should be able to?

Cali didn't want to dwell on the doubts running through her mind. So far, Nick's confidence had remained strong. It radiated through his firm grip as he continued to hold her hand, and she was determined to keep the confidence she had gained from him, from slipping away.

Flashing blue lights appeared in front of them. Two cruisers sat parked on the road, but no one was in sight. Nick parked behind the cruisers and started to get out, but hesitated when Chad spoke.

"Let me out. I can show you where they are, Sheriff. You'll never find them on your own."

"Then it's a good thing I'm not on my own, isn't it?"

Chad's gaze smoothed over. Now, his features revealed nothing. No emotion showed through. No hatred. It looked as if he had mentally retreated, pulling himself away from reality.

Nick looked at Cali and his voice softened. "Are you ready?"

Cali's pulse leapt; she hadn't expected him to ask her to go with him. "I'm ready."

They climbed out of the truck at the same time. Nick walked around the front and put his arm around Cali, tugging her to his side. "Let's go get Serena."

Chapter Twenty-Six

Cali wasn't sure what she was seeing at first. The darkness swallowed everything farther than three feet ahead. The driving rain didn't help her vision either. But, a moment later, flashlights appeared ahead of them. Two of them, directing bouncing rays of light to the wet, sandy ground. Two human forms appeared, then the shadow of another emerged, huddled close to the others. As Cali and Nick made their way down a sand dune, the people drew closer. She recognized Deputy Owen from his lengthy stride, and he was carrying something. Or, someone.

"Serena!" Cali broke free of Nick's grasp, running to meet the two deputies.

She nearly ran into Deputy Owen in her haste to get to him. Nick caught up and shone his flashlight at the woman in Owen's grasp. It was Serena, and it looked as though she was asleep. "Is she...?"

Owen said, "She's been drugged, but she's spoken to me already. She's confused, but knows her name."

Relief overcame Cali, and she expelled the breath she had been holding. She tasted salt on her lips before she realized she had started to cry. She glanced at the woman huddled beside Deputy Castle. Marlene Stanton's short, dark hair stuck out in all directions, and she ducked her head against the strong winds. They continued to walk toward the cruisers as Cali turned her attention back to her friend.

Nick took hold of her hand, lacing his fingers with hers. "Let's get her to the hospital," he said, urging her back toward the road.

When they arrived at the truck, Nick switched Chad to Deputy Owen's cruiser, freeing enough space for both Cali and Serena to ride in the back seat. Cali climbed in, and Deputy Owen placed Serena next to her. Serena drew open her eyes, blinking several times. "What's going on?"

Cali's silent tears turned into deep sobs. When she could speak, she said, "It's so good to hear your voice again. You're safe now. It's over."

Serena seemed to understand, although she was not fully awake, and relief registered on her face for a moment, before she leaned over and fell back to sleep.

Nick climbed into the driver's seat and twisted around. "We've notified the hospital. They'll be waiting for us."

"I can't believe it's finally over. We did it Nick. We found her." Tears continued to stream down her face. Cali leaned her head back against the headrest as the adrenaline, which had fueled her body for the last several hours, drained away. Exhaustion claimed her, making her more emotional by the minute.

It would soon be time to go home. Somehow, the thought was not as appealing as it used to be. Going home meant leaving Nick. A new kind of anxiety seeped its way into Cali's system, dampening the tremendous joy in finding Serena. Cali's gaze met his intense, deep-blue eyes as he glanced into the rearview mirror, and she wondered if he was thinking the same thing.

Chapter Twenty-Seven

Cali's damp palms rested on the hard, wooden armrests of the hard, wooden chair in which she sat. She looked around Nick's office, thankful the sheriff's station had emergency backup generators. The lights were dim, but sufficient.

She focused on her surroundings while waiting for Nick to finish speaking with Helen in the main room. His office looked the same as the first time she had entered it, but it felt different. The sense of organization was still there, and the bare essentials remained occupying the desk, but now that she knew the man behind it all, it felt welcoming instead of intimidating.

Fatigue blurred her vision, and she rubbed her eyes to clear them. She checked her watch, but it had stopped working, probably from being drenched for most of the night. She looked around Nick's office for an indication of the time, but found none. She figured it was well after midnight by now, and her energy reserves were fading fast.

Chad and Serena had been admitted to the hospital for treatment—Chad for burns, and Serena for dehydration. Marlene was still in good physical condition, but they kept her overnight as well, based on the trauma she had undergone in her ordeal.

Nick had insisted Cali let the emergency room

doctor take a look at her, and she had earned a bandaged shoulder for complying. She had a sprained shoulder, but luckily nothing had been permanently damaged. She had wanted to stay in the hospital with Serena, and it took both the doctor and Nick to convince her Serena needed to rest.

When she and Nick returned to the station a few minutes ago, Helen had greeted them at the door with hot coffee and a warm smile. Then, she hugged Cali, surrounding her with much needed compassion. Cali had nearly broken out in a fresh wave of tears at the friendly gesture.

Cali stood and paced Nick's office, wearing an extra pair of his clothes, which he had given her before they left the hospital. His sweatpants gathered around her ankles, and kept slipping at the waist, although she tightened the drawstring and hiked up the legs repeatedly. The T-shirt hung down close to her knees, but she couldn't think of anything else she would rather be wearing at the moment. Nick's fresh, soapy scent clung to the material, and she enjoyed the comfort it provided.

A pang of loneliness hit her as she remembered again that now that they had caught Chad, she would be leaving soon. Nick had been so busy dealing with the aftermath of tonight's events, he hadn't said anything about what was to come, and Cali wondered if it had crossed his mind.

"I want you to get some sleep." Nick's deep voice shook her out of her thoughts as he entered the office.

Her pulse leapt and she turned. "What about you? Your eyes are bloodshot. You look exhausted."

"I'll sleep soon enough. I want to get you settled first."

"Where?"

"The worst of the hurricane is over, but I think it's best if you stay here tonight. We'll check on my cottage first thing in the morning, but for now,

Deputy Owen has a couch in his office. It sleeps well."

"You sound as if you know from experience."

A smile tugged at the corner of his lips. "I've been known to work long hours on occasion."

"Really? I hadn't noticed," she replied with her own smile.

He shrugged, and took her hand in his. He led her to Deputy Owen's office. "I'll go grab a pillow and blanket for you. We have brand new ones in the storage closet."

"Where will you sleep?"

"We have emergency cots. I'll set one up in my office."

"And Helen?"

"She'll probably insist on staying up through the night. I'll be right back."

Cali hadn't been alone for long before Deputy Owen peeked in the door. "May I speak with you for a moment?"

His question startled her. She turned to face him. Dark circles ran under his eyes, and his usual arrogant smile had deflated, leaving a solemn expression on his features. He held his lips drawn tightly together as he waited.

"Of course."

He stepped inside the office and shut the door, offering her a seat.

Cali opted to sit in the chair next to the door. Still uneasy about being alone with Owen, she wanted to have access to the exit. "Nick said I could sleep here. But I don't have to if you'd rather…"

He waved his hand. "It's fine. That's not why I wanted to talk to you." He pulled another chair from behind the desk and sat in it. He ran a hand through his tussled hair and met her eyes. "I'm sorry." His long, narrow face held traces of regret.

Cali consciously kept her mouth from dropping open. "Sorry?"

Owen shot a pointed look at her bandaged shoulder. "Chad Livingston found you because of me."

She leaned forward, surprised by the remorse in his voice. "Deputy Owen, I don't think…"

He held up a hand. "Please, hear me out."

"All right." She settled into her seat, waiting, and fighting to keep her head clear enough to focus. She tried to hold back a yawn, but couldn't.

He blew a deep breath into the air. "I shouldn't have told Lex Harrison where you were staying. He led Livingston directly to you."

"Chad would've found me anyway."

"It would've taken him more time."

"Yes, but…"

"Why are you defending me?"

Good question. She should be mad, but for some unexplained reason, she wasn't. Cali had to think about her answer for a moment before she realized the truth. "Because I don't want you to feel guilty for something someone else did. Chad kidnapped me, Deputy. You didn't. I spent too much time this past week blaming myself for something he did." She leaned back in the chair and crossed her legs.

"You're not going to let me feel bad about this are you?"

"I don't want you to feel bad about it. I just hope you learned you don't need publicity and fame to be important. Nick thinks highly of you. That says a lot."

"Nick used to think highly of me. But not anymore."

"It may take some time, but I'm sure you can regain his trust."

"I hope so. I'm sorry I let him down."

Her opinion of Owen started to rise. "Don't forget you're the one who found Serena."

He nodded, stood from the chair and crossed the room, looking more uncertain than she had ever seen him. "Thanks for not being angry with me. I'm beginning to think Nick's been right all along."

"Been right?"

"You are special."

Her stomach dropped and the room began to spin. Chad had called her special. Nausea rose inside, and she was glad she was sitting down. "Nick told you that?"

Nick stepped into the room. "I told you what?"

****

Nick stood in the doorway to the office holding the pillow and blanket and waiting for a response. Cali's cheeks paled right before his eyes. "Chad used that word." A shiver passed through her. "He used it as an excuse to stalk and kidnap me."

"What word?"

Deputy Owen cleared his throat. "Sorry. I didn't mean…"

Growing irritated at not knowing what they were talking about, Nick stepped farther into the room and tossed the blanket and pillow onto the couch.

"I'll just go check on Helen." Owen stepped around Nick and left.

Nick turned his focus to Cali. She avoided looking at him. He was tempted to demand she tell him what they had been talking about when he caught the glimmer of tears in her eyes. The last thing he wanted to see was more tears. He had seen enough tonight to last him decades. First Cali, then Serena and Marlene. Even Helen had let out a few. His guilt returned, and he didn't even know why Cali was starting to cry again.

She walked to the couch and sat on it. Picking up the pillow, she asked, "How long do you think it will take?"

"Cali, you're confusing me." He ran a hand through his hair as fatigue and frustration tugged at him.

She stared at the floor. "How long will it take for me to stop hearing his voice? To stop smelling his lime-scented sweat? To stop seeing his distorted features every time I close my eyes?"

Her whispered words instantly erased Nick's agitation. "It's only been a few hours, Cali."

"How long before one word will stop bringing me to my knees?"

"What word?" Nick eased down beside her.

"Special. He said I was special." She lifted her gaze back to his. "I still feel the nausea that struck me when he used that word. The way he said it." She shivered and hugged the pillow to her chest, but not before Nick caught her pulse going wild at the base of her throat.

"He can't hurt you anymore." He wanted to take her in his arms, but the defensive look in her eyes held him back.

"I'm not so sure about that."

He scooted closer. "I have two deputies guarding the door to his hospital room. He's cuffed to the bed. He'll be locked up in a cell where he belongs as soon as he's well enough."

"Do you think he'll ever get out?"

"Not with the DNA evidence, and yours and Serena's testimony."

"I can testify, but how can Serena if she was drugged and doesn't remember anything?"

"She remembers enough. She figured out Livingston was giving her the drugs through her drinks. So, she pretended to drink them, and acted like she was drugged. She nearly escaped once."

"But Serena was drugged when Deputy Owen found her."

"Livingston made her drink a soda laced with GHB while he watched. She had no choice that time."

"How do you know?"

"She woke up enough for me to talk to her for a

few minutes earlier in the hospital." He leaned closer and took her hand in his, rubbing warmth back into her fingers. "She said Chad didn't touch her."

Cali's eyes rounded in surprise. But, she still held a hint of disbelief in her gaze. "He didn't?"

He shook his head. "Serena said he was distracted after he took her. He wasn't at home much for the first few days. Then, she said he kept talking about you." Anger surged through him at the thought, his protective instincts sprang to life again, and he shifted her hand closer.

"What about tonight? She was knocked out." She shivered, and goose bumps broke out all across her skin.

Nick released her hand, picked up the blanket and draped it across her shoulders. "She was examined at the hospital. There's no evidence she was..." he trailed off when Cali looked away.

"What about Marlene?"

"I don't know. She's not ready to talk much about it yet."

Cali appeared as if she wanted to know more, but fell into silence. She blinked a few times and rubbed her eyes, wincing when she lifted her right arm.

"How's your shoulder feeling?"

"It's swollen and sore."

Another fresh wave of anger surged through Nick. Cali had been hurt by the High Tide Stalker, and he hadn't been able to prevent it from happening. He lifted her hand and kissed it, then turned it over and traced circles on her palm with his thumb. He closed his eyes. "He had you, Cali. The stalker had you. What if...?" He cringed at the images flashing through his mind.

"I'm OK, Nick. Look at me."

He did.

"I'm safe. You arrived at just the right time."

She softened her voice as a smile played at her lips. "You know, for someone who doesn't want to be a hero, you're pretty good at it."

"I never said I didn't *want* to be one. Only that I don't have everything it takes to be one."

"Maybe not on your own. But with God's help, you can do much more than you ever could otherwise."

His heart beat at a clipped pace. "You truly believe that, don't you?" He held his breath. Waiting. Hoping. Had he really found an incredible woman who shared his beliefs, values and faith?

"Yes. I…"

"You what?"

She took in a deep, shuddering breath. "When Chad kidnapped me, I prayed."

He waited, drawn in by her sincere words.

"The prayer we said together that night, in your cottage. I asked for courage, serenity and…"

"Wisdom," he said along with her.

"And He followed through."

A tear slid down her cheek, and he traced it with his thumb. He wanted to kiss her. He wanted to take her in his arms and keep her there. But, he reminded himself she would be leaving soon. "I guess you'll be glad to be going home to Brookstone, and the family business."

Cali avoided his eyes.

He let go of her hand, and stood. He took a tissue from a box on Deputy Owen's desk and handed it to her.

"Are you still asking me to go home, Sheriff Justice?" She blew her nose and locked her gaze with his.

"I'm not asking, Cali. But we both know it's going to happen. Coral Isle is my home, and Brookstone is yours."

Helen appeared in the doorway, drawing his focus away from Cali. "You'd better be getting some sleep, Sheriff." Motherly concern deepened the creases at the corners of her eyes. She stepped back and left, not waiting for a reply.

Nick glanced once more at Cali before walking to the door. "She's right. You need sleep, too." He hesitated with his hand on the light switch. "We both knew this was coming," he whispered as he turned out the lights and stepped away.

Chapter Twenty-Eight

Knowing a situation was coming, and actually being there were two entirely different things. Reality hit Cali hard as she stood in Nick's cottage, folding her sundress and stuffing it into her duffle bag. With the strained events of the past week, her emotions couldn't take much more. Now that it was time to leave, she felt as though she had reached her breaking point.

She sighed, rolling her right shoulder to relieve the ache. Two days had passed since the night Chad had abducted her. Two long days of answering Nick's questions, sitting by Serena's bedside listening to her telling what had happened while she was in captivity, and dreading leaving Nick and Coral Isle behind.

Thankfully, the hurricane had spared Nick's cottage. Too bad her car didn't have such luck. It had floated up the street and been left half buried under the sand. At least she had good car insurance coverage.

Nick had exhausted himself trying to help the residents of Coral Isle get their lives back to normal, and it looked as if it would be weeks before they were finished. Out-of-state contractors had piled onto the island to remove the debris that littered the streets, and the power company had enlisted outside help to repair the damaged power lines.

Cali hadn't seen Nick since that morning. After having her fill out police reports, he had dropped her off at the cottage and left again. She already missed him.

Her cell phone rang, and she realized she had been staring at nothing, lost in thought for a few minutes. Cali checked the caller ID. "Dad." She had called him yesterday to let him know Serena had been found, but she hadn't had a chance to have a real conversation with him.

"Hi." Cali made an effort to sound cheerful as she answered the phone.

"Hey yourself, hon'."

Comforted by the familiar sound of her father's voice, she said, "That's the closest you've ever come to actually saying hello."

"Oops. I must be slipping. I'll have to be more careful. I wouldn't want to have to start saying goodbye."

She laughed, relaxing her tense muscles. "Serena's doing well. She's going to be released from the hospital later today. Nick's promised to drive us both home tonight."

"Good. I'm anxious to hear the details of what's been going on over there. And, I'm looking forward to meeting Nick."

"Yeah. He's great..." her voice trailed off as sadness enveloped her.

"Something's happened between you two," he stated, rather than asked.

"I love him, Dad." She held her breath, waiting for his reaction.

"I know."

"You do? How?"

"Fathers have instincts about these things. Wait until I tell your mother. She'll be dancing for days." Excitement tinged his voice. "I have to admit, it's about time you settled down."

"I'm not that old."

His raspy chuckle warmed her. "I sure hope not. 'Cause that would mean I'm *really* old."

"Aren't you forgetting something?" Cali asked as she walked out of the bedroom, heading for the sliding glass door. She slid it open and stepped out onto the porch. The beach was filled with tourists once again; the hurricane hadn't kept them away for long.

"Aren't I forgetting what?"

"I'm coming home. I have a life in Brookstone. Nick's life is here."

"So, what are you going to do about it?"

Cali lifted her brows. "What do you mean?"

"If you're worried about me and your mom, don't be. We managed the Herald before you came along, and we'll manage without you."

"But I..."

"And, I'm sure Serena will understand too."

"Understand what?"

"Why you've decided to move to Coral Isle."

"I have?"

"I've known for the last year you've been restless. You haven't been content working at the Herald for a while. You didn't think I had noticed?"

"I didn't even realize how unhappy I was until I came here."

"And found what you've been searching for. Am I right?"

"W-well..." she stuttered, stunned at her father's insight. "I have been thinking about doing something someone suggested I do."

"Which is?" he prompted.

"Help create public awareness to try to prevent people from falling victim to criminals. If people would be more alert of their surroundings, that would be a great start in protecting themselves." Excitement rose in her, along with her voice. "People tend to relax and put their guard down while on vacation. I can think of dozens of ways to try and keep that from happening."

"That's my girl. Now, you go and tell Nick what you've decided to do. I'm sure he'll be thrilled. And remember, I still want to meet him tonight. He can't keep you yet. Not until he marries you."

"Dad." Heat filled her cheeks, and overflowed to the tips of her ears.

"You heard me. Now, finish packing." He disconnected the call, again, without saying goodbye.

Cali paced across the porch, working her nerves into a frenzy. Could she move to Coral Isle and start a new career? A new life? Her life in Brookstone had been the only one she had ever known. But, her dad was right; she had been restless for quite some time. Was this the opportunity she had been looking for?

Lord, how do I know what you want me to do? Is this what you have planned for me? She understood the only way of being truly content was to follow God's plan for her life.

Excitement tumbled through her at the thought of filling the void she had been experiencing for so long. She looked at the beach, and drawn to its serenity, shut the sliding glass door and walked down the stairs and toward the ocean.

The hurricane had cleared the air, leaving the sky bright, crisp and clean. Although the temperature was high, the humidity had decreased, leaving a much more comfortable environment. Her feet hit the ground and she looked at all of the sand and debris that had washed up under Nick's cottage, cringing at how much work it would take to restore.

She climbed what was left of the ruined sand dune, and walked toward the ocean. Several yards to the right, the remnants of a neighboring cottage lay scattered across the beach. A few stilts remained, a skeleton of what used to be before the high water surge swallowed the cottage.

Sympathy washed through her and she prayed,

Lord, please help the people of Coral Isle recover from the hurricane's destruction. She shivered, knowing Nick's cottage could have been destroyed too.

Cali turned her focus to the ocean, letting the now calm waves soothe her as she thought of the choices that lay ahead. *Lord, where do I belong?*

"Hey." Nick's voice vibrated through her, shocking her system. She couldn't remember the first time his presence had affected her so easily, but if today was any indication, she was lost to him. No other man could even compare.

Cali turned as he approached, her nerves becoming as tangled as her wind-tossed hair. She met his sparkling eyes, and had the answer to her question. She knew where she belonged. She only prayed Nick felt the same.

A smile sprang to her face as she looked him over. "You wear your uniform well, officer." She glanced down the length of his clothes, her gaze stopping on his shiny badge. "Of course, it's the man underneath it who I can't seem to resist."

A smile tugged at the corner of his lips. Then, his gaze landed behind her and his smile faltered. "It's a shame so many cottages were lost in the hurricane."

Cali struggled through her anxieties and said, "It is a shame, but God takes bad situations and makes good things come from them."

His focus shot back. "I recall telling you the same thing a few days ago."

"You did tell me. And now I've seen it happen."

"Why do I get the feeling you're not talking about the scraps of wood lying scattered across the beach?"

"Because I'm not." She tucked her hands into her pockets to keep Nick from seeing them shake. She wished she'd had time to plan what she was going to say, and to plan how to approach the subject. But, she couldn't let the opportunity pass by. Gathering what bit of courage she had, she said, "I want to propose to you." She choked on the words that tumbled from her mouth. "I-I didn't mean... I meant...I, uh..." Her face heated as if she had been in the hot sun all day.

Nick's features registered surprise, and a broad smile spread across his face. He waited in silence for her to continue.

Taking a deep breath, she said, "I want..." Her eyes strayed to his lips.

He took her hands in his and stepped closer. "You want?"

Focus, Cali.

She closed her eyes and opened them, hoping to reset her wandering mind. "I want to raise public awareness by founding a program about safety and how to avoid falling victim to criminals." She rushed through the words in one long breath.

Nick's sudden look of admiration sent a boost of confidence her way. "That sounds like a great idea. I'm sure the people of Brookstone will benefit from it."

"I wasn't talking about Brookstone. I was talking about here, at Coral Isle. Nancy Chandler mentioned something about writing articles to raise public awareness. I thought I could take it a step further by working closely with the Coral Isle Sheriff's Department. That way I can reach so many more people."

"Working closely with the department?" His voice came out low and gravelly, as a new intensity darkened his eyes.

Cali's heart thumped in her chest, drawing Nick's gaze to the pulse at the base of her neck. She swallowed. "Yeah. Closely."

"That would mean?"

"I'd be moving here," she hesitated, "to Coral Isle." She held her breath, waiting for his reaction.

His features lifted, but only for a moment. He

rubbed the nape of his neck and expelled a deep breath. "Emotions are volatile. I want you to think through this before you make a decision. You would have to give up your life in Brookstone." His tone became businesslike as he studied her.

"I have been thinking. I've wanted a change for a long time."

"How do you know this is the right one? Cali, a lot has happened in a short amount of time."

"Are you trying to talk me out of it? You don't want me to stay?"

"I want you to stay. What I don't want, is for you to have any regrets. If you make this kind of decision based on emotions, you may be disappointed later."

Suddenly, Cali understood his hesitation. "Disappointed in you?" *Not a chance.* "I'm not looking for a hero, Nick."

"That's good. Because as I said, I'm not perfect."

"And I'd never expect you to be." The breeze carried a strand of hair into her eyes. She absently brushed it aside, already accustomed to the constant wind from the ocean. "Honestly, I think God has been preparing me for this for a long time."

Seconds stretched into minutes as he seemed to contemplate her answer. His grin returned, and then lifted into a full-blown smile. "OK."

"OK? That's it? No more input?" She had hoped to hear more of his opinion, but had a feeling from the smile on his face he approved of her idea.

"I think you have the right motivations."

"I do?"

"Yes. You're trying to follow God's plan for your life. I couldn't ask for anything more. But, there is one thing you should know."

"What's that?"

"When it comes time for a proposal, it will be my job."

Adrenaline spiked through her system. A

nervous laugh escaped her lips as he closed the remaining distance between them.

"When it comes time?" Cali managed to ask.

Nick lifted a shoulder. "Call me old fashioned, but I'd like to win your father's approval first."

Cali couldn't breathe. If only Nick knew he already had it.

"Any ideas how? I want you to be my wife, Cali."

Her heart skipped a beat, and the last of her doubts melted away. Her knees felt weak, and she would have sunk right into the sand if he hadn't reached out and caught her. Cali leaned into his embrace, and lifted her gaze to his. "That's easy. Use your finesse on him."

Laughter erupted from deep in his chest, and he leaned down for a soft, lingering kiss. When he pulled away, he asked, "How do you know it will work?"

She grinned and answered, "It worked on me didn't it?"

Epilogue

Two months later...

"I never thought I would be getting married barefoot." Cali wiggled her toes in the sand. A wave of cool ocean water washed up over her feet as she looked at Serena standing beside her.

"That's reason enough to get married on the beach if you ask me. Who needs high heels anyway?"

Cali laughed. "Do you think everything will go as planned? We haven't had long to put this together. I didn't think I would be this nervous, but I can't seem to stop worrying about everything. What if the weather isn't as nice as the forecasters are calling for tomorrow? What if...?" Cali wrung her hands, shifting her feet in the sand.

"We did plan this wedding in record time, but whether it all works out the way you have intended it to or not, the important thing is you're marrying a man who is crazy in love with you. Look at him." Serena interrupted Cali's fears and motioned behind them. "He can't keep his eyes off of you."

She followed Serena's gaze and her heart pounded wildly in her chest. Nick stood several yards away, just outside the ring of fire blazing on the beach. Sure enough, his gaze locked onto hers, and he dazzled her with a broad smile.

"I love having the rehearsal dinner on the beach. The bonfire adds a romantic touch don't you think? I only wish I didn't have to wait until tomorrow to marry him," she said to Serena wistfully, returning Nick's smile with one of her own.

"Who says you have to wait?"

Cali's gaze snapped back to Serena. "We're only rehearsing this evening; tomorrow's the real thing."

"It's your wedding, if you want to marry him tonight, do it."

"You've lost your sanity. Come on, we'd better go mingle with the others before Pastor Nelson gets here and things start rolling."

"Things are already rolling. Look," Serena commented as Nick's young nephew, Charlie, barreled into him from the side. Nick fell over and rolled in the sand with him, laughing along the way. A tickle fight ensued, and Nick held his hands up in surrender.

"He's a good man, Cali. I'm so happy for you." Serena placed her hand on Cali's arm. "I know I've said it before, but thanks for doing what you did to find me. Not many people would have put themselves in danger for me. I've been looking for a way to show my gratitude, and I think I've just found it." Serena walked toward the group of relatives and friends mingling around the fire.

"Found what?" Cali hurried to catch up with Serena, but Donald Stevens stepped into her path.

"Hi, hon'."

"Dad! I didn't see you."

"Of course not! The way you've been ogling your intended, I had to jump in between you two to get your attention." He gave her a brief hug, his gaze filled with humor. "Your mother is in Nick's cottage hunting for tissues. She's so happy she's been crying for weeks."

Cali sobered. "Dad, you know I'll miss you and Mom."

"Nonsense. We'll only be three hours away. Your mother and I will be around so much you'll get tired of us."

"I could never get tired of you. Just remember I can still help you out with the newspaper from time to time."

"I'll keep that in mind. But, I have a feeling you're going to be quite busy from now on." He glanced at Nick. "Between moving, adjusting to married life and a new career, I don't think you'll have much spare time."

"I'll always have time for you, Dad. I love you so much." Cali gave him another hug.

Nick's voice came from behind. "Mr. Stevens."

Cali stood back as the men shook hands. The approval in her father's eyes sent a wave of warmth through her. Nick slipped his arm around her waist, sending a stronger wave of heat down her spine. She reached up and brushed sand from Nick's shoulders as she looked between the two men she loved most in the world.

"I want you to know I'll take good care of her sir," Nick offered.

"I know you will son, or I wouldn't let you have her." Donald Stevens clapped Nick good-naturedly on his shoulder and ambled away, but not before Cali noticed tears gathering in her dad's eyes.

She took in a shaky breath as she scanned the crowd gathered on the beach. With all of the wedding preparations, and the emotional rollercoaster that went along with it, Cali felt tears threatening her own eyes. Seeing someone she loved become emotional was a sure way to make her own tears start flowing.

Nick turned her to face him, and she wrapped her arms around his neck.

"I can't wait for you to be my wife, Cali. These last two months have been the best, and longest of my life." He leaned close, dropped his head and slanted his warm lips across hers.

One set of hands started clapping, and then others joined in. Cali's face heated to a full flush as she pulled back and faced the crowd of loved ones cheering them on.

"We'd better go join them." Nick released Cali and took her hand in his, giving her a gentle squeeze. "One more night, baby." He shot her a promising glance that heated her to her toes.

They strolled to an empty beach chair, and Nick sat, pulling Cali along with him. He wrapped his arms around her and hugged her tight. The gentle breeze added a slight chill to the autumn air, and she snuggled deeper into his embrace.

Sparks from the bonfire blew high into the air as Nick's father added a few logs to the blaze. The smoke wound its way into the sky, lazily shifting with the wind.

Mrs. Mayes sat directly across from them, watching them with a knowing smile as Helen sat talking with her. Cali caught a few snippets of their conversation—something about a new pie recipe Helen intended to bring in for her 'boys' at the station.

Helen glanced at Nick and said, "If you like my new recipe, I'll give it to you and you can bake it for Cali sometime." Helen gave Cali a playful wink.

"I'd like that," Nick's deep voice rumbled beneath Cali's ear, and warm waves of comfort washed across her.

Nick's pastor came strolling up to the bonfire, and she physically tensed. "Pastor Nelson's here. It's time to get started with the rehearsal."

Nick ran his hands up and down her arms. "Relax. This is supposed to be fun, remember?"

She turned in his arms to face him. "I want to make sure everything goes well, and that everyone has a good time."

"You just make sure *you* have a good time.

That's what's important."

"I'll try to remember." She started to move away.

"Not yet." Nick hugged her tighter. "This is about you and me," he whispered.

Drawn to him, she leaned in for a kiss. His hand wrapped around the nape of her neck as he encouraged her to continue. The sounds of the conversations around them became muted, as all of Cali's senses focused on Nick. His warm, strong arms held her close, while his lips tantalized her with promises of what was to come.

Something crashed into them, knocking Cali out of Nick's grasp and off the chair. She blinked in surprise as she found herself lying on the cool sand, under the attack of a five-year-old. Charlie knew just where to aim, and he began his assault. He went for her ribs first, tickling her until she broke out into peals of laughter.

She rolled across the sand with him, targeting the underside of his bare feet. The innocent giggles coming from Charlie pushed away Cali's nervousness and provided her with a much needed distraction. All at once, her nerves abated and she began to fully enjoy the evening.

"Charlie!" Casey's high-pitched voice came across the sand.

Cali looked up in time to see the apologetic look on her soon-to-be sister-in-law's face. "It's OK Casey. Charlie knew just what I needed." She hugged him close and managed to get in another round of tickles before Casey gently urged Charlie to his feet.

In the past two months, Cali had become friends with Casey and William and had fallen head-over-heels for Charlie. His sweet smile and wide brown eyes had captured her heart from the first time she met him.

"Come on, honey, go wait with your dad. It's almost time to start," Casey said.

Cali watched the two walk away before bringing

her gaze back to Nick. His approval showed through his wide smile, and love shone through his eyes.

She was about to climb back into his arms when she glanced at the guests and noticed groups of the men and women whispering to each other. She gave Nick a quizzical look, and he shrugged saying, "I have no idea."

She rose to her knees, brushing sand from her hair, arms and hands. "I think Charlie would have gotten the best of me if Casey hadn't come to my rescue."

"I taught him well." Nick teased. "Come here," he said, leaning forward to take her in his arms.

As Cali reached Nick, Deputy Owen came walking out on the beach, carrying the large wooden cross Nick had built for the ceremony.

"What's he doing?" Cali asked.

"I'm not sure." Nick released her and stood. "Owen," he called, "we're supposed to set that up tomorrow."

Owen ignored him as William joined in helping him stand the cross upright, burying a few feet of it in the sand for stability.

Nick opened his mouth to speak again, but his father approached them. "Nick, come inside with me. I need to discuss a few things with you."

Nick's parents had arrived home a few days ago, welcoming Cali into their family as if she had been a part of it for years. Although Cali was still adjusting to Nick's father's stern personality, she had bonded with Nick's mother from the first moment they met.

Serena appeared behind Cali, and tugged on her arm. "Come with me. I want to steal you away for a few minutes."

Cali stood, dusting sand from her jeans. She glanced at Nick, who looked as confused as she felt. All of the other women had disappeared inside the house. "What's going on?" Suspicion rose in her as fast as the waves crashing into the shoreline.

"You'll see," Serena and Nick's father said at the same time.

Cali smiled hesitantly as Nick shrugged saying, "I think we're outnumbered." He indicated the group of men heading their way with Charlie in the lead.

"All right, I'm coming." Cali let Serena whisk her away as she spared one last glance at Nick, who flashed a quick smile in her direction before becoming surrounded by Deputies Owen and Castle, Nick's father and William.

The men had completed their task, and the cross stood straight and tall on the sand, casting long shadows across the beach as the sun began to set. A narrow pedestal filled with white roses and green ivy stood near the cross, holding the decorative unity candle Cali had hand picked.

"My candle. It shouldn't be out here overnight." She struggled against Serena before adding, "And my roses—the wind will blow them away."

Serena said nothing, only continued pulling her toward the cottage.

"Take it easy. I'm coming...I'm coming." She gave up trying to deter her insistent friend.

Her heart warmed as she glanced back once more at the cross, and looked at the sandy area in front of it where she would become Nick's wife. When she nearly stumbled, she returned her focus to Serena.

The knowing smile on her friend's lips made Cali's heartbeat kick up a notch. When they reached Nick's cottage, Serena led her to the porch. They passed by the caterers setting up the buffet for the rehearsal dinner on the first level.

"Everything smells and looks so good." Cali reached for an appetizer, but before she could grab it, Serena stopped her. "No snatching."

"But..."

"Come on will you? They are all waiting for us."

"All who? Why?"

Serena didn't pause until they came to the top floor, where Cali had gathered her wedding supplies. "This is it." She slid the door open.

"This is what?"

"Back here," Cali recognized her mom's voice calling from the bedroom as they walked in and slid the door shut.

"What's going on?"

Serena said nothing as she pulled Cali along behind her. When they reached the bedroom, a hush fell over the group of women standing around Cali's sheer, white wedding dress.

Mrs. Mayes leaned on her cane with a satisfied grin on her face, and Helen stood wringing her hands. Cali's mother dabbed a tissue at her eyes as Nick's mother stood next to her, beaming. Casey smiled and fidgeted behind the others.

Cali's gaze roamed over the group as she waited.

Her mother stepped forward. "Try on your dress for us, will you, dear? I want to make sure everything is absolutely perfect."

"I've tried it on ten times already. It fits..."

Serena sighed. "She's your mother. Just do as you're told."

"OK. I surrender." Cali held up her hands. "I don't know what this is about, but I'll humor you."

Cali swept the dress from the bed and changed in the bathroom. When she emerged, gasps crossed the room.

"You look beautiful."

"How darling."

"Oh, it's just lovely."

Cali wasn't sure who said what, as they all spoke at the same time, but she warmed with the compliments. "I knew this was the dress I wanted from the first time I saw it."

"It's new," her mother commented.

"I know. I bought it," Cali said quizzically.

"And this is old," Helen said bending and

clasping an ankle bracelet on Cali's left ankle.

"This is blue," Casey said, holding a beautiful hair clasp in her hands. She reached Cali, armed with a brush. "I'll just show you what it looks like." She began combing through Cali's long, wavy hair.

When Casey finished, Cali looked in the mirror. "I like this better than the way I had planned on wearing my hair for the wedding tomorrow. Thanks Casey. I think I'll..."

Before she could finish her sentence, Nick's mother said, "Here dear, try on this lipstick. You don't need much, just a dab will do."

"O-OK." Cali applied the rose-tinted lip-gloss.

"Just perfect, dear. You look lovely."

"Thank you." Cali felt a blush rise to her cheeks.

"That's about it, isn't it ladies?" Helen asked as she looked around at the women for confirmation.

"About it?" Cali asked. "Will someone please tell me what's going on?"

Serena stepped up to Cali. "Don't forget something borrowed." Serena lifted the silver necklace from around her neck, watching the outline of a heart swing back and forth like a pendulum.

Cali remembered how thankful Serena had been the day she received it back. "I'm so glad you have your necklace again."

"Would you like to wear it for the wedding?"

Tears formed in Cali's eyes. "I'd be honored."

Serena slipped it over Cali's head, laying it gently on her neck. "I believe that does it. Something old, something new, something borrowed and something blue."

"Thank you so much. Why don't you all keep these things until tomorrow? I'm afraid I'll misplace them."

"You don't need to worry about that," Serena said with a smirk.

"I don't?"

"Nope. Because, you're getting married tonight,"

Serena stated simply.

"*What?*"

"You heard her," Helen said in a matter-of-fact tone.

"I-I can't."

"Why not?" a chorus of voices asked.

"Everyone who was planning on being here tomorrow is here tonight," Cali's mom said.

"And we already have food," Helen spoke up.

Mrs. Mayes added, "The pastor's here."

Cali's initial confusion began to fade. "How do I know Nick would want to?"

"Well…" Serena stepped forward. "If you walk out on that porch, and take a look at the beach, I think you'll have your answer."

Cali swung her gaze from one woman to the next. "How long have you ladies been planning this?"

Serena glanced at her watch. "Oh, about an hour. Ever since you said you wished you could marry Nick tonight."

Cali's mouth dropped open. "I said that but I didn't really think," she paused, "I was just…" She thought for a moment and her pulse began to race. "Do you think we could?"

"Let's find out." Helen wrapped an arm around Cali, walking her toward the door.

Cali could only hear the loud thumping of her heart as Serena ran ahead to slide the door open.

"But what if…"

"Nonsense. Move it, Cali. He's waiting for you," Mrs. Mayes said, thumping her cane on the floor. "I've waited years for this moment, no need to keep me waiting any longer."

Cali took a deep breath and let it out slowly. She took one step toward the porch, and then another. She passed by the couch where she had cuddled with Nick, and fell in love with him as they said the Serenity Prayer together. Tears blurred her vision as she remembered how she used that same prayer to escape the clutches of a maniac, and how she had learned to trust God amidst all of the chaos.

As she stepped onto the porch, wind-blown sand dusted her bare feet, and the gentle breeze caressed her face. The salty sea air welcomed her, as the setting sun cast brilliant orange, yellow, and purple ribbons of color across the darkening sky.

She walked to the railing, grabbing it for stability before daring to look at the beach below. Her gaze swept across the sand dunes.

She had her answer.

Nick stood at the foot of the cross, handsome in his tuxedo. His gaze locked onto hers and a broad smile spread across his face, as he waited patiently to become her husband.

Thank you for purchasing this White Rose Publishing title. For other wonderful stories of romance, please visit our on-line bookstore at www.whiterosepublishing.com.

For questions or more information contact us at info@whiterosepublishing.com.

White Rose Publishing
www.WhiteRosePublishing.com

CPSIA information can be obtained at www.ICGtesting.com
Printed in the USA
BVOW030243300312

286460BV00006B/5/P